i cope

Copyright © 2016 Harold Abramowitz
All rights reserved.
#RECURRENT Design & Cover by Janice Lee
Cover Photograph of Raymond Hotel: Courtesy of the
Archives, Pasadena Museum of History
ISBN - 978-1-937865-72-6

The #RECURRENT Novel Series is an imprint of
Civil Coping Mechanisms and is edited by Janice Lee.

For more information, find CCM at:

http://copingmechanisms.net

Blind Spot
by Harold Abramowitz

for Levia Pearl Abramowitz

Table of Contents

Part I - Hotel	8
Part II - Funeral	76
Postscript - Night	154

Part I - Hotel

1

Failing to notice, and he put his hands out, flexed his fingers. There were lemons in the trees, and, at that point, there was not much else about himself that he had to imagine. Just don't think. It will come. Just don't think. Still, that was flat thinking, and that was abusive behavior, and yet, this is what he ended up telling himself. There will be a war, a mistrial declared. Someone will have heard me. I was not myself. I wanted to scream, to be a better man. And it continued that way for hours. There were hours, then, hours in the dark. In the dark of the hotel. And in driving for hours to get to the hotel there had been smoke, and fire, and there had been something else. A tragedy that befell the world. A real and singular tragedy that would come out of the blue and befall the world. So much of it was made up. And this was in the summer, and there was no one else in the room. There was red in the room, however. And there was a pipe left on a table. And there was the sound of his heart beating. I knew I lived somewhere. He'd left his hat on the table. But what he couldn't have known was the one thing he might have found disturbing. He had to slow down.

———

There is trouble in the room. He is looking around the room, trying to find his way back in. And, in a minute or two, there will be a sound, his signal, and then there will be somewhere to go. But these events have to take place in a room.

———

At the end of the street, and I thought it was like music. I thought it would be more like noise. I thought of many things, and those things that I thought of continued to bother me. I was at the end of my rope, the end of my tether, and that was the way they dressed things up in those days. It was a beautiful summer's night. The air was cool. The hotel was a very beautiful place to be. All of the other guests thought so too.

———

And then he tells himself a story.

———

But I kept seeing the things that I was seeing, and the things that I was seeing were not mine. I had a bit from a book, and I had a bit from a story that I'd been told when I was very young.

———

There was someone waiting for him in the lobby. He'd gone downstairs and was having a drink at the bar. He'd waited near the hotel lobby, waited in the bar just off the hotel lobby. He had the key to his room in his hand. He walked in the cool night air, and there was a breeze, and this was right at the beginning of events. It excited him to no end, realizing he'd come to the right place. And the hotel was, indeed, just the right place. For the first time in his life, he'd understood. He'd seen enough signs to know. Still, this was new, this was drinking at the hotel bar, and waiting.

———

These are the rules of the game. There is no spitting on the floor allowed, and when the General begins the discussion, the gentlemen will remain in their seats and act with the utmost consideration to one another and to whomever has the floor at any given time. There is a discussion beginning, another discussion beginning, and then, later, someone will draw the curtains back and the music will start. Then there is the sound of the car, and the sound of the wind through the car windows. It is cool there for a summer's night, even on an early summer's night. It is a night unlike any other night. He is walking down the grand staircase. He is in a hotel. He tells himself that the setting is fine, even if stories have been set in hotels before. He is walking down the stairs on his way to dinner. The food, so far, has been excellent. The food has been much better than expected, and this, inevitably, leads him to think of the drive to the hotel. He'd thought out his stay at the hotel in the car. His itinerary. He thinks of many things while he is in cars. This is because he has recently had to drive a lot. He has been driven a lot. And then he is at dinner and seated among the other guests. And this is valid criticism. Yet, this is also the type of criticism that stings. Still, at that point, he is able to tell the other guests a thing or two about the way he thinks a top-notch hotel should be run. After all, he has his opinions, and his opinions are as good as anyone else's, he feels. And then he pauses briefly, and smiles, and clinks his glass with the person sitting on his right. The other guests are very charming. He thinks of the time when he was ill. At one point he'd had a serious illness, but that was long ago and he is feeling much better now, thank God. And then there is laughing. And a rustling in the bushes. This, however, comes as a shock, as a complete surprise. Is there someone laughing at him? He has, after all, just taken the Lord's name in vain. And then there is fear, and then someone, one of the other guests, perhaps, does something that upsets him. And he is afraid, afraid that they, the other guests, will not want him for himself anymore.

———

A man in a tuxedo. A man in a long fur coat. A man with a gun in a hunting jacket. A man in a smoking jacket.

———

The hotel was set in the mountains, set high in the mountains. The hotel was well known as a place to go for cures for one's ills. The hotel was set atop a great mountain range, and he turned his head. It was the laughing that upset him most. A mocking sort of laughter, and, yet, it had been amusing, had been amusing right up to that point to be at a hotel. It had been amusing and it had been urbane. A civilized thought. A concept. An idea. The point he'd wanted to make. And, if he thought about it, the point he'd been trying to make, to express clearly, to the other guests in the dining room. And, pity, because, in general, the hotel was a place he could have remained happily, for a time, if only he'd refrained from thanking God. There, and he'd said it again. I feel better, thank God. Yes, thank you. I am doing, feeling, much better now. I am much better now.

———

The hotel was very large and very old and very discrete, in its way. Expensive. A place to go for people who wanted to get away from it all. A place to come, famously, for people to cure their ills. He sat in a chair in the lobby and read a newspaper and smoked a cigarette. Cigarette smoking was still very fashionable in those days. When the hotel was built. There were pictures on the walls. And his room made sounds. Yet, it was not the type of hotel one would bring, say, a family to on vacation. A very large hotel. But the stairs were there, and so was the lobby, and his room was there, and so was the lounge, and then the grounds outside, and the dining room, and the halls, and the bar. So far, all of the necessary elements for a hotel. Yes, the location would do. It would serve his purpose, even if it was obvious, and even if it had been done many times before.

2

And, even so, it may have occurred to him, at that point, to try something new. There was a face, maybe a face, or really a pair of eyes, that stared at him from just inside the bushes. There was a beautiful and mysterious face hidden behind the door of his room. And when he entered the room, he put his hands out, flexed his fingers. And this was the way it had often been in the past.

———

A man in a long fur coat stood at the top of the grand staircase and sang a popular song.

———

The hotel sat at the edge of a forest, a desolate forest. It was a place to go for people who wanted to get away from it all. Desolate. Far from the city. Far from any city. The hotel was a large and complex structure, a structure replete with many rooms and many floors and many secret and hidden places. And on the day he first arrived, he noticed, one could not help but notice, the hotel's massive size, its enormity and complexity.

———

There was wind. There was wind, and there was, he believed, at least one other guest in a room somewhere on his floor. Perhaps, in the room right next to his. From the window in his room, he could see the moon, and then a star in the sky. He sat in a chair and smoked a cigarette and read a newspaper. There was something circling in the sky overhead. It was a bird, or it had been a bird, and in the garden there had been a cool breeze. It had been in this yard, or in a garden in this yard, that he'd first seen something move, move about freely, or it had been in this yard, or in a garden in this yard, that he'd first seen something else, something else entirely. A pair of eyes. The garden was beautiful and he sat on a bench. The bench was old and very comfortable. He sat on the bench and crossed his legs and felt the wind and felt the sun until the sun disappeared behind a large wrought iron gate, disappeared behind a bank of tall trees. There was nothing more he could do. He got up. But it was all such a long time ago, and there were people in the garden with him, and there were people in the hotel lounge, now and then, who he was, sometimes, friendly with.

And, after a moment, he stands. He stands up and walks out of the lounge and into the hall, and while this occurs, almost simultaneously while this occurs, someone else, one of the other guests, perhaps, enters the lounge from the hall. It has been a useless day, mostly useless, and even sitting outside has not helped alleviate the feeling that this day has been, somehow, mostly useless. He'd sat in the garden and had not relaxed. It had gotten cold very quickly. And then, at that very moment, a man in a long fur coat coughs, or clears his throat, and then sings. Coughs, or clears his throat, and then sings a popular song. And there is someone, something, special waiting for him in his room. He is in love again, or he is young and in love again with someone special, with someone he's just met. It isn't a large garden. The garden only occupies a small portion of the yard. There are plants and flowers, of course, and a few decorations, a turtle, or, to be precise, a stone turtle. There is something passing overhead, maybe a bird, and it becomes increasingly clear that the other guests have left the lounge.

There is much talk about luck, or chance, or good fortune, in the dining room that evening. The other guests seem to be in an uproar, a slight commotion, because someone, once, had either won or lost a great deal of money, somewhere, at roulette, or while playing at another gambling game, perhaps in a lottery. The dining room is a little louder than usual tonight, and there is a slight commotion because, apparently, someone had, once, either won or lost a tremendous amount of money, somewhere, while gambling, while playing at a game of chance, at roulette, or in a lottery, perhaps. There is laughter and there is smoke in the air. It is a spectacle of sorts. Luck, or chance, as he passes through the double doors and into the dining room. He is among them, the other guests. He has found himself among them, the other guests. And, at that point, he is either one among them, the other guests, or he is nobody, he feels.

———

At night, the forest is lit by moonlight, at least partially, or, to be specific, only the very edge, or border portion, of the forest, the edge, or border portion, visible from his window, is lit by moonlight, or it, the forest edge, or border portion, is lit by lights from the hotel, indeed, it is often, on most nights, very hard for him to decide exactly which light is responsible for the view, his view, the view from his window, of the lit edge, or border portion, of the forest, and sometimes, the hotel gardens are lit at night for special occasions, and this light must be considered as well, and then he will ask himself whether or not anyone really and truly notices him, loves him.

———

He sits at the dining room table, and the table itself seems to be familiar, in some way familiar, and there are other guests at the table. Still, he is not sure, at that point, whether or not the seating arrangement will prove to be at all in his favor.

There is a knock at the door. It is at that moment, when he is sitting in a chair in his hotel room, smoking a cigarette and reading a newspaper, that he hears a knock at the door. The door is old and made of a very heavy wood. Like much of the hotel, the door has a natural, or rustic, look, is designed to give a natural, or rustic, impression. There is a knock at the door. The knock is slow, or sounds slow, in a way, through the heavy wood. There is a knock at the door, and he doesn't get up. This is in the hotel. The hotel is large and old and quite beautiful. It is a structure, a building, that could never be duplicated, that could only have been built during the time in which it was built.

There is a knock at the door, and he gets up to answer. He opens the heavy wooden door, and there is no one there. As expected, there is no one standing in the hall. There are lights on in the hall, the lights are always on in the hall, and there are the sounds of the lights in the hall, but, at that point, there is no one standing outside his open door.

3

Wood was falling. And it was like a dream. The dream of a peasant, or of sky, or of some other mythic figure. He didn't stop to ask. There were no stars in the sky, and no one knew his name. But it, the non-dream, crumbled, came crumbling down. The hotel was in the mountains. It was far removed from the city, and there was nothing else around it for miles. The other guests enjoyed themselves during the daytime. They hiked and visited lakes and rode on horses. It was years ago. And he sat in his room and smoked a cigarette and read a newspaper. There was something, someone, next to him. Not necessarily a person, but something. And when the world turned, and when things were slow, there was trouble, inevitably trouble. Senses were hidden. And there was nowhere to go. And then, on the third day, a piece of paper, a number, was slid under his door.

In the room. He'd waited in his room, and then there was a dream he'd had. He'd never had a dream before, and he'd have to start all over again, thinking about the dream he'd had. He sat in the back of the car and tried to sleep, but sleep wouldn't come, and then there was the roar of the engine, the loud roar of the engine. The engine was loud, and its roar oppressive, and he wondered how anyone could stand the sound of an engine up close. And this was when there were no trains allowed, and there was a mysterious hotel set high on a mountaintop, and he was a guest at a hotel.

He wore a raincoat as he walked along a mountain road. He'd arrived by car and had exited the car too soon. There was a radio in his room. And there was a clock in his room. And there were cats that lived, that roamed freely, in and around the hotel. And, after several days, he became friendly with the people, the other guests, at his table. He'd been assigned a seat, a specific seat, at a table. There was an arrangement made, and things start slowly, sometimes. He sat at the table. He sat at his seat at a table in the dining room and did not speak to the other guests, other guests with whom he'd grown friendly. He was fond of the other guests, of the other guests in the hotel, even though he had never spoken to any of them. There had been a fire in the hotel, once, notoriously, many years before. A hotel had burned to the ground. A large structure, made of wood, had burned to the ground. The fire had occurred during the off-season and, fortunately, there had been no deaths and no injuries, but the hotel had burned to the ground. The hotel, the old hotel, had been large and complex, a masterpiece of construction and design.

In death, there were two of them. Partners in death. The saga of a hotel. The places they went. There was a home, a house, in the middle of the forest. And there was a place deep in the woods where lovers sometimes went. The hotel fire had not, officially, killed or injured anyone. But deep in the woods there had once been a cottage, a hideaway, a place for lovers to go. And there was listening. And the sounds would have shaken him. There were the sounds that the trees made, and there were the most important nights he could imagine. One day, this will all end. There will be fire, and this will all end.

It was in the old hotel, and there was a wedding, and there was a circus, an entire circus had been hired for a wedding party. A bride and groom and dignitaries and other guests. In the time before the fire. The lamps were lit. There was the sound of an enormous party taking place. He could hear the party through the walls of his room, through the floor and through the ceiling, through his open window. The party sounded like a groaning or a moaning. The moaning or groaning of, perhaps, a wounded animal. He was tired, and the radio was off. Once, the radio had been something of a necessity. Indeed, there had once been a real need for radios in the world. There was a very large radio in the lounge, still, and the other guests, the men, mostly, would gather around the radio and stand and listen and then, later, have important, sometimes heated, conversations with one another over drinks and cigars.

The hotel was a marvel of design and a marvel of luxury. Boxes and trunks and various other types of luggage were brought up the mountainside in cars. The trees swayed up and down the driveway. And he woke up feeling like himself. He woke up feeling well. The hotel was renowned as a place to go for cures, cures for one's ills. The hotel was set high in the mountains and transportation was difficult. There were no airplanes, and this could not go on. If he had to remember what he had to remember, then there was no point in its going on. After the world had ceased to exist, after the plans had all been executed, then maybe he could rest. Redemption would come, and so would something else. But the idea of thousands and thousands of people, that many people at one time. Still, the General would get excited, become increasingly excited, as he always did, and after one too many drinks, and after one too many cigars, the lounge would stink and the atmosphere would change, change, would never be quite the same again. He didn't want to think about ghosts, however, and he didn't want to think about anything else. There was supposed to have been a cure, and, by then, there was supposed to have been a real and tangible change in the way the world looked.

He took a hike. He walked in the mountain air. There was moonlight. The moonlight was beautiful, and it was never daytime, and there was never anybody else around. And, at some point, something would have to change. It, however, excited him to think about a past he couldn't remember. It didn't excite him at all, and there was nothing to think about, and no one to ask. Time moved forward. There was little to think about, and he would close his eyes. At night, he would close his eyes, and the answers would come. Answers would come to him the way answers always came to those who wanted answers, and then he would be through waiting, and then the future would start, and then the future would be bright and there would be very little to worry about, new worries, yes, but not the same worries.

———

On the night of the fire, the people screamed. There was screaming and there were noises and the old hotel burned to the ground. No one was sure how long it took for the hotel to burn to the ground, but the flames lit the sky for many, many nights.

———

And if only he'd listened. If only he'd been there. Save the people. Save the people from what they really needed to be saved from. It might have changed everything. Redemption. Retribution. And, ultimately, he didn't know which, which to choose, which way to go. And then the General lit his cigar and thoughtfully, carefully, addressed the men in the lounge.

———

There was a real feeling, a strong impression, that he'd been in the dining room before. He recognized the table. He'd managed. He'd finally managed to find himself in that place, and at that time, among a certain segment of the population, the other guests, people, indeed, what most would have called the right kind of people.

The old hotel had been a marvel of luxury and design. Thousands had been employed, had been involved, in its construction. The old hotel was enormous and, yet, had burned to the ground in a single night. The work of many. Thousands. Destroyed. Destroyed in a single night. He dialed a number. The telephone booth was just outside the bar, close to the hotel lobby, not far from the grand staircase. He could observe the grand staircase and, if he turned his head, part of the lobby from the telephone booth. He covered his ear with his hand to better hear the operator. The operator asked for the number, for the name of the country he was calling. He talked on the telephone. The number was in his coat pocket. He pulled a scrap of paper out of his coat pocket. He held the paper in his hand, held it out in front of him. He gave the operator the number. There was a war. There was always a war somewhere. Specific wars that required specific plans and lots and lots of communication. The General shook his hand firmly. He was glad to meet him. He said he was glad to meet him. He said he had come to the right place, once and for all. Once and for all, he had come to the right place to meet people.

4

Lifting his way up the mountain. Change. The view is superb, he said. It is even limitless, in a sense, to look up beyond the top of the mountain, the entire range of mountains, and see what I can see. But if there was no light, it might be better, it might be better still. As an old soldier would say. Or if it was something else, not merely a prediction, but rather, a divination, or, perhaps, something else again. Yet there was something about the old man, the General, that couldn't be placed. There was always a deep sense of discomfort about him, a feeling that this man would never stray. Stray. The whole concept of straying was foreign to him, was, somehow, too much. He stood in the hall outside his door. This was early in his stay.

There are bargains to be had at the bottom of the mountain, Sir. Real bargains. And the trading just goes on and on forever. It was a vegetable, of course, some type of vegetable, not an animal at all, nor the course of the road through the jungle or forest, but, instead, a quiet mountain road, a village wouldn't have been out of place. But when he sits in his chair and finishes his cigarette and folds his newspaper in half. When he lies in bed and thinks of the whole course of human history, the events of the day, then the idea of a kind of magnum opus becomes very appealing. This thought, of course, turns him into a kind of monster, and into a kind of magician as well. Then there is a question of his knowledge, of the types of things he knows. What he wants to be when he grows up, what his loved ones have told him to do. And he's amazed at how well he remembers their lessons. Reasonable lessons. Not afraid of the big, bad world at all.

———

There is a room in the hotel, a strange and secret room, that seems too small for a person to live in. It is too small. There has to be more room there. There has to be more room if a person is to live, and there has to be a way out of the room, too. The soldier, or General, if that's what he is, laughs. If he's really a soldier, or General, he laughs. And what else? If it isn't a sense of freedom that he's after, then what else? This is his time of rest. There is no one of particular interest, no important guest, staying in the hotel at that time. And, at that point, he doesn't have much work to do, but the life he's been leading is not as easy as it appears. It is, in fact, hard for him to find a way to relax. This is a hotel. The other guests arrive at the hotel all day and all night. It is a never-ending stream of arriving. There are certain dignitaries, other guests, important people, in the hotel at that time, at all times, it seems. The hotel. The hotel is no longer as full as it had been. It has shut down for the season. And in the past, the hotel had done better business, in the past the hotel had attracted a better clientele. This was once a very famous hotel. An elegant and famous hotel, far from the city, far from any city, a hotel set high in the mountains, set against a picturesque backdrop of natural trees and meadows, not at all far, in fact, only a short distance, from quaint villages and restful and therapeutic forests and rivers and streams, indeed, forests and rivers and streams that teem, all year round, with abundant wildlife, game.

———

As he leaves his room, he sees an old soldier. The bell rings and it is time to get up. There are several activities in and around the hotel that he wants to join in that morning. This takes place during the build-up to the war, to a great disaster, or during the aftermath of the war, the fire, of a great disaster. It gets so complicated. He has to look around to remember where he is. He has to remember his name. And, at one time, his fingers were more nimble. There was a square, and he used to visit the square and sit and drink coffee, or, more often, tea, in the café on the square. Now, people do things for him. Now, he is waited upon. And, because of this, he has lost some of his freedom, some sense of his freedom, and then the world turns upside down, and then there will be a disaster. A large disaster will occur, whether or not he, or anyone else, knows it, and whether or not he, or anyone else, expects it.

He is not at home. At one time there was a home. A red roof, and, at first, the world supplied him with a kind of vision, and then it merely ended up surrounding him, surrounded him because of the onset of an unexpected disease, a malady, an epidemic of sorts, or surrounded him simply because a new point of view had taken hold, the way new things sometimes take hold. He took a trip deep into the forest. The deepest part of the forest was only a short distance from the hotel, from his room in the hotel. He'd given it his all, he'd given it his best shot, he'd sat in a chair and smoked a cigarette and waited. It was in the hotel that he first saw the General, or, to be specific, he'd first seen the General in the hotel, first, in the hotel lounge, or, first, on one occasion, when the General had swept down the grand staircase. The General swept down the grand staircase and into the lobby, and, at that moment, he felt he had a confession to make. There was something powerful and moving in his heart that he felt he would like to have confessed, if given the opportunity, if given half the chance. It was in the hotel. The hotel was set high in the mountains. Orders, too, had come from the highest levels. And he'd had to do what he'd been told. He'd had no choice. And that was before, when there was still a great deal of passion involved. Now. Passion. Not knowing causes. What it will cause. Causes that inspire a great deal of hope, produce, manufacture, hope, and that is all. And this is not known, this is, ultimately, an unknown quantity, a quality, an unknown, and, at this point, he is filled with its emotion still.

———

Soon he would be spending the night in a hotel. He was soon going to go on vacation. There were many friends in those days. There was much to do. There was much to observe, to look after. And if he wakes up in a strange bed, and if there is music coming from the floors below, music coming from the ballroom, or from the dining room, perhaps, or coming from the lounge, well, then, what of it? It was the smell, but not really a smell, more like an odor, perhaps, or the thought, really, of a particular vegetable that woke him up, that disturbed his sleep. And, at that moment, it was almost revealed, there was almost a revelation. The truth would be told and everyone would know the deep secret that had, until that point, been kept hidden. It looked bad for him, at that point. The whole company had been knee-deep in it. There was no knowing if they'd escape. And he was held somewhere. He had been separated for who knows how many days. He'd been held in a kind of makeshift holding place, a place that resembled, that was like, a prison or jail cell. Barely a place, carved out of the jungle, carved out of the forest. And this was most respectable, by the General's account, of course. It was going to be a good ride. All he had to do was sit back and enjoy the ride, sit back and listen. There was a word, almost a word. And the word itself was almost a revelation. To follow one's own advice. How it would be best to just sit back and enjoy the ride. And, after a moment or two, he puts his hands out, flexes his fingers. He was feeling most alive. He has to raise his arms so his hands, his fingers, will not swell. The room is very small, too small for a person to fit in, to live in, comfortably. And then, for some reason, there is a stop in the action. The General will not rise this time. This time, at this time, he will not rise at his table, or in the lounge. At this time, the General, if that's what he is, will not rise and salute his comrades-in-arms, the fallen, the lost, with a cigar and a glass in his hand, not this time, for some reason, not at this time.

It is quiet outside, on the grounds of the hotel. The gardens are, in fact, very well kept. There are swans and ducks and horses and pigs and even rats. The forest is full of animals. It is a wonderful place to rest, to take a holiday. But this particular spot is very difficult to find, very exclusive, and once one leaves, it is very difficult, if not completely impossible, to return to. But the season has ended, and this is the General's advice. The season will end and most of the other guests, and most of the staff, will leave the hotel. And, in fact, there are only a few other guests and staff, a skeleton crew, so to speak, who will remain at the hotel during the off-season.

5

Rest. It was the ocean, simply the thought of the ocean, that caused the suicide. A change in luck, or fortune. He was running up a mountain path, and not complaining, never stopping to complain, not like all the others. On the back of his plate, there was a wire. A wire, or a thread, or a small something else that could just barely be seen. Sharp. And it was something sharp, wasn't it?

―

Because of the way things changed, the way things changed so quickly, it almost surprised him when he was bad, when he was not as good as he could have been. He thought of her in the car on the way to the hotel. The red, or green bag, the pair of glasses. It was enough. It was cold in the car. The air was thin. There was someone in the room with him. He hadn't thought of his mother for many years. It was a vacation, and he needed rest. He had been hiking. He held his head up. He remembered standing in the sun. He remembered he was at work and leaned up against a wall and tried to rest. There was the sound of an automobile horn, the sound of many automobile horns honking at one time. Other guests were arriving in a never-ending stream. And, in those days, there was always the sound of laughter at the hotel. There was always some reminder of the way things used to be, of the way they used to be done. And if there were wires, electricity, the wires were kept well-hidden. And it was not a joke, not this time, not at that point. It was not a joke in the lounge, or in the dining room, or at the bar.

―

He lifted his hat and ran his fingers through his hair. He ordered a drink at the bar. It was a time of panic. The people, the other guests, on the streets, or at the hotel, couldn't believe their eyes. Something had to be done. And it didn't hurt, did it? In the end, the future didn't hurt that badly, did it?

He walked out of his room and into the hall. The hall was long. The hall was covered with plush carpeting for as far as the eye could see. And there is someone in the darkness, or the darkness is bothering him. He can see a slip of light from under the door, or rather, a slip of paper on the carpet reflected in the light from the hall. The lights are always on in the hall, and this light, or a similar light, used to bother him when he was at home alone.

It was always after midnight. He was sure of that, but he was not exactly sure what time it was. Being a modern hotel, the clocks are designed to blend seamlessly, unnoticeably, into the decor. There are no clocks, and no names appear on the hotel registry. There is, however, a sort of code. All information regarding the hotel guests, important or otherwise, is written in a sort of code. There was the old way, of course, the way that was depicted, or rather, described, in all the books. The book he'd read had said so. He was certain that he'd read at least a description of the hotel, the old hotel, in a book, once, long ago. And it was true. This was thinking, research. Learning! The whole process was satisfying, in a way. Like completing a puzzle. And there was an agreement, or rather, an arrangement, made. The men would welcome him into their regular company in the lounge. They would offer him a cigar and a drink and a chair, and they would ask him important questions, questions he would, usually, be able to answer. And it really was as easy as that. It was as easy as sitting down in the chair and settling in when the evening began, as easy as getting up out of the chair and exiting the lounge when the evening was over. In fact, the chairs were very comfortable in the lounge.

The General always stood when he spoke, which meant that he was almost always standing. Time slowed. In fact, he couldn't tell what time it was, at least not at that point.

And there was a dance that night in the main ballroom, and flowers in vases had been set on tables all around the hotel. The flowers were very aromatic. They smelled extraordinarily good. Indeed, the hotel had been designed to give a natural, or rather, rustic, impression.

There is a terrible volume to the suit he wears that night, in its many colors, in the way it rests on his shoulders. Your size. Your size. And I especially love the General. He's such a wonderful man. So funny, in a way, in his own way.

During this segment of his vacation he is usually able to say something smart and, more importantly, perhaps, original to the other guests. He is, in fact, usually able to contribute in a positive way to whatever conversation is occurring in the dining room at any given time. There is fresh fruit in bowls on all the tables in the dining room, fresh fruit laid out for the guests in exactly the same way each morning. There is nothing quite like, or quite as wonderful as, the smell of fresh fruit in the morning, he feels. Things are getting better. He walks down the stairs and enters the lounge. It is morning, and there are only a few other guests, early risers, like himself, present in the lounge at that time. It is morning, and the company in the lounge is mixed, both men and women. The men and women are reading newspapers and magazines, or, rather, there are men and women, other guests, hidden behind newspapers and magazines in the chairs in the lounge. In the meantime, he has overheard a conversation. He is almost certain that a conversation has taken place in the kitchen, or that a conversation has taken place in the hall, near the kitchen. He is almost certain that a conversation has taken place between the chef and one of the assistant chefs, between two of the chefs, certainly, or that a conversation has taken place, somewhere, between one of the assistant chefs and someone else, perhaps one of the other guests.

———

His signal, or rather hotel bill, had come to him in the form of a letter, or note. The letter, or note, containing his signal, or rather hotel bill, had been slid under the door and was waiting for him when he entered his room that night. He was certain, however, that he would not be able to accept the invitation. There is no tomorrow. Don't accept the invitation. Accept the invitation, or there is no tomorrow. There is no future anyway. No future. And, at that point, he holds his hands out, flexes his fingers. He is seated at the dining room table. He smiles, and clinks his glass with the person sitting on his right. The other guests are very charming. During this season, there are fresh cut flowers placed on tables all over the hotel. It is late spring, and the flowers are cut each morning in the mountain meadows, meadows that are common in the area immediately surrounding the hotel. Mountain meadows that, in fact, provide a picturesque backdrop that the hotel guests, by and large, seem to enjoy, indeed, seem to, consistently, marvel at. The flowers are freshly cut each morning and brought to the hotel in large carts. They are very aromatic. The flowers, in fact, smell wonderful, and he often finds himself standing next to, or sitting at, tables set with vases of flowers that give off a wonderful aroma. He is afraid. There is the wonderful aroma of freshly cut flowers in the air. He wonders what he will do next. He fears that he works too slowly. In fact, time seems to move more and more slowly as the date of his vacation begins to draw near.

6

The air was refreshing. It lifted his mood, and he took that to mean the air was cold. There was a sense in which he waited. He waited and waited. He waited in the cold air on the grounds outside the hotel and wished for good luck. It was an absence, however. And, in fact, exactly the type of absence that normally would have bothered him. An absence of good news. The absence of a sign, of some kind of sign, that would appear and guide him. There was a bird in a tree, but, at that point, the bird in the tree did not mean that he was happy. He did not take the bird in the tree, the fact of a bird in a tree, as a sign, or symbol, as any specific sign, or symbol, or as an indication of anything at all. Yet the absence of any specific sign did not disrupt his thinking, it was just that a sense of purpose, his sense of purpose, or self-esteem, was, at least temporarily, lost. It was cold that week in the hotel. There was no reason to believe otherwise. And in the room, he waited. In fact, he chose his words carefully. And there was good reason for him to have been careful, someone might have been listening. And the night-bird sang, and he could hear the night-bird's song through his window.

———

There must have been some mistake, for some mighty, or towering, figure of authority had been brought down, somewhere, and there was red in the room, and his running all around the lounge and not finding a place to sit. The radio was on. It had been an emergency situation, and the radio was on. His car had broken down, or rather, the car that had been driving him had broken down. It had been a long day. Still, there was a lot of emotion in the way he went about his business. It was the most interesting day yet. And he put his hands out, flexed his fingers. He was feeling rather happy, as happy as he could possibly have felt under the circumstances, and then the car had broken down. He was desperate to find a place to sit. It seemed that he would again have to spend the night in the car. In fact, there was no question that he would again have to spend the night in the car. And the hotel was grand. It was impressive. It sat high on top of a mountain. Indeed, the whole area surrounding the hotel was somewhat dominated by the hotel's size, by its grandeur, by its enormity and complexity.

The rest of the day was strange, had been strange as well. There was dreaming, and then there was remorse, and then there was a sudden understanding, or misunderstanding, of what had drawn him to the hotel in the first place, of what it had been that had drawn him to the whole idea of a hotel in the first place. And it might have been that, that understanding, or misunderstanding, that had destroyed the car. And it might have been just that because in those days anything was possible. In fact, everything had begun innocently. And this is merely to say that, at that point, he hadn't yet arrived. He hadn't yet arrived at the hotel.

It was in the room. He was in his bedroom. He was in the room, and he'd just begun to write his autobiography. The story of his life would be written by him, and it would be written correctly.

He needed a break. He needed rest. The work was hard. And after just a week or two in a hotel.

He could have, conceivably, written his autobiography, his magnum opus, so to speak, anywhere, just because it was something he'd always wanted to do.

There were lemons in the trees. The lemon trees surrounded a gated garden. It was a beautiful garden, and one hidden away. Indeed, there were many beautiful, secret, and mysterious spots, hidden gardens, and the like, in and around the hotel grounds. The old hotel, too, had been famous for its hidden gardens, its locked gates, its hidden paths, and for its very restful atmosphere. It was a beautiful day. There was a gentle breeze. And this was right. This was the right way of doing things, slowing down, going on vacation, even if the vacation was, actually, an assignment, or, rather, work. And it had been the General who'd shown him how it was done, how these things could possibly be made to work together. The way he stood with his cigars, and his voice, with his seemingly infinite supply of funny, always very funny, jokes and stories and anecdotes. This was living. This was life. This was life the way he'd always imagined its being lived. Living. Not going where he had to go. Not forcing things. But things. What things? And why were there always so many things to consider? And questions. And why were things not fluid? Not the way things were supposed to be? Of course, this is not about money. It was one of the General's favorite lines. Of course, this is not about money. But one had to be around him to understand. One had to be a member of the General's inner-circle, his cavalry, his clique, his company, his coterie, his cellblock, so to speak. And then there was always laughing. And then the truth might take a long time to come forth. And the hotel was beautiful. It was set high in the mountains, near restful lakes and streams, not far, in fact, from beautiful forests and expansive and therapeutic meadows. And this was a fear of his, the fear that the truth, the slow coming of the truth, would take up his whole vacation, take up his whole day, and then the tragedy, not to mention the tragedy, that was sure to follow.

There is snow falling in the mountains. There is a mysterious song, a once popular song, that can be heard through his open bedroom window. His room has a window. He sleeps with the window open. It is a quaint and beautiful hotel, an old hotel, set high in the mountains and designed to have, to give, a natural, or rather, rustic, feel. The hotel's atmosphere is indeed quite idyllic, in its way. And each day, and night, is reaching its capacity. Each day, and night, is reaching its point, its own unique threshold, he feels. And, from time to time, the mountain air seems to cause something miraculous to rise from deep within him. For instance, he is certain that the birdsong is a sign. He is certain that he is angry, and he is certain that he thinks about the General too much. On occasion, he has caught himself thinking about how the General, specifically the General, would react to what he is thinking and saying, specifically, to what he is thinking and saying about himself at any given time. But this whole line of thinking is without virtue, has, in fact, very little to do with virtue, he feels. And, as a result of this, there is, indeed, a sense, then, in which he is, as it were, all alone. A sense in which he sits and waits, and sits and waits in a place where there is no hope of his ever being seen or recognized. This is a hotel. He is in a hotel, and thus there is a question of the hotel's authenticity, of its truth and accuracy, of how well it succeeds in presenting itself. Is there even electricity in this hotel? But the fact that the hotel did indeed possess electricity had been irrefutably established at a much earlier time.

And as he stands on the veranda and looks out over the beautiful scenery, the mountains, the paths, the trees, the lakes and streams, the cottages and meadows, he is happy he has come here, happy he has come to this place. The lure, pull, of the mountains is eternal. There is no break in the harmony, and no seeing anything but for what it is. There is the singing, the constant singing of birds, and the sounds, intermittently, and at other times, of animals. All can, in fact, be described there, he feels. He could conceivably describe it all, but he has not written a postcard for a very long time. He has not told anyone where he is or what he's been doing for a very long time. And he is, in a sense, at work because of this. Despite his being on vacation, he is at work because he is, after all, on assignment. Indeed, he is in a place he was ordered, or rather, instructed, to come to, to arrive at, for a very specific reason.

———

There is someone, another guest, perhaps, in the next room. There is, it seems, someone, another guest, perhaps, staying in the room right next to his.

———

In fact, his time at the hotel has been long and productive. He has even been honored many times during his stay. He has dined at the General's table, with the General's wife, and with the General's many aides-de-camp and frequent visitors, other guests, and this despite the fact that his seating assignment in the dining room was, at first, not as favorable as one might have wished. Yet it was his good fortune, in this way, in this very specific way, as luck would have it. Or rather, an inevitability. The General. Still, he was seeking something in particular that day, some sign. And the bird sang. And all of it seemed familiar, somehow exceedingly familiar, in a way.

7

The deceptions of ghosts, or not of ghosts, or not of anything at all. It was peace that sustained the war. A matter of oppositions. And in that discontinuity, that continuity, because it was reversible, he stood and watched as the other guests entered the hotel. They, the other guests, entered the hotel through the lobby. A never-ending stream. And there was home to think about as well. A thought as definite as any other. The moment he left his room. And this trouble. Really troubling thoughts. When there was something at stake, some matter of honor, or another, something specific to the war, or to war, in general, at least. It was in the room that these thoughts occurred to him, provoked him, tiny thoughts, not even the thoughts he'd intended to consider. And there was a kind of absolute silence spawned by, perhaps, a deepening sense of victory, or rather, of entitlement, and yet, there was no stage, no stage specifically, nor even a place for the guests to go and be entertained, still, they, the other guests, seemed to eat a lot.

In the garden. There was a seat in the garden. There were several seats beside him in the garden. It was a beautiful day. The sun was out and the birds were singing in the air. A home in the forest, so to speak. And all men require a home in the forest. At one time, and those were, seemingly, days of greater purity, men lived in the forest. There was no violation. There was no particular code of honor that had to be followed. It was simple, really, the men, the other guests, lived in the forest for a time and then they left and continued with their lives, their businesses, their personal development, and so on.

It is in this way that the days continue. He is alone in a hotel. This is neither a break nor a vacation, not exactly. He is on assignment. He is at the hotel for a specific reason. Or he is on leave for a specific reason. In either case, he is not living his usual schedule, not performing his usual tasks and duties in their usual ways nor at their usual times. In fact, he has had to call home. His vacation has lasted longer than expected, and this, this situation, his condition, the condition he finds himself in, has already caused unimaginable problems for the world, for the world at-large. It has already caused a great deal of consternation and pain and suffering. And luck or ill luck or bad omens have had nothing to do with it. It is pain. There once was pain. He is lying in bed in his hotel room. It is a perfect night. He is high in the mountains. The air is sweet and the atmosphere is ideal. All his pain will be absorbed by the mountain air. The aroma, the simple smell, of trees, and of flowers, living flowers, and of air, clean air, will help heal him of all that ails him. It is this benefit, one among many, that the hotel offers, that the hotel is, in fact, famous for. He remembers this fact. The memory of this fact comes to him suddenly. It is something that pulls at him while he drives the car, or, rather, while he is driven in a car. The hotel he is to visit will be beneficial for him. Then the car breaks down. There is a problem with the car and he has to pull over to the side of the road, that is, the driver has had to pull the car over to the side of the road. The car is large, but it appears to be in good condition, if a little old and not quite in the current style, or fashion. There is a pen is in his hand and he is about to write a letter. He has just finished writing a postcard.

There is a certain anticipation as the car winds its way up the mountain road, a certain sense of curiosity as the car approaches the hotel. The hotel is large and laid out in a very complex way. There is a real, almost indescribable complexity to the way the hotel is laid out. And, in fact, he is not sure, at first, that he belongs in such a fashionable place, or among such exclusive company. The hotel is very elegant and very famous for its proximity to certain curative regions, specific areas that seem to cure people of what ails them. The hotel is beautiful and expensive, and the guests, generally, stay there for a very long time, often for consecutive seasons. As he stands and watches the other guests enter the hotel, he is aware of how easily they are accommodated. How easily the hotel, in its massive size and complexity, is able to absorb them, other guests who arrive in a never-ending stream, and then no sooner seem to disappear. This is the miracle of the hotel. Of all hotels? Of this hotel in particular. It is part of its mystery and fascination and charm. This information, of course, pertains to the old hotel, to the one that burned to the ground. Still, there is a question of trouble. Specifically, the trouble of blocking out certain stimuli. And the question becomes the hotel itself, or, rather, it becomes a game he plays in the hotel. He is standing in the hall. He is standing next to a small table in the hall. There is a vase filled with flowers on the table. He is at his seat in the bar, the seat from which he is able to observe the lobby and the grand staircase. He is outside the lounge. He is in the lounge. He is in his room. He is eavesdropping on the guests in the room next to his. There is, of course, a form for all of this, an unspoken language, and an unguessed at consequence. And this consequence, of course, depends on his actions, on how, and in what manner, he will choose to carry himself. And this line of thinking inevitably leads to his next decision. The spontaneous decision that will propel events to their conclusion. It is already a conclusion of sorts that has just occurred. This meandering of his. This standing around the periphery of the hotel. He is standing in the hall, and this, too, has its consequences. A change that takes place unexpectedly. A rapid deployment of his qualities of service. There is, of course, much more to be said. And it, also inevitably, will be said at some point. But here it suffices to become the picture, the display, so to speak, of a kind and gentle turn of events. Of a barely spoken of purpose, of points of fact, and then of their contraries. What occurs is occasional.

There is a peculiar resistance on his part to contact, to unexpected social contact, especially. And despite the weather, the weather had been nice, and despite the unseasonable and difficult weather, it is really the season that he finds himself responding to. That and particular voices. Not so much their content but the quality, timbre, of the speech itself. And this causes something to change within him. A change of perspective that can only be characterized by its utter lack of perspective, or of joy, or of any other quality, positive or negative, that he can imagine. It just is what it is and there is no telling what form it will take from one moment to the next. Essentially, it is in his power to make mistakes, it is his right to have come to this place in spite of his intention, of his clear intention.

8

That night, he will sit in the lounge and be in the company of the men, inevitably in the company of the other men, other guests, in the hotel, or, rather, in the company of the men, the other guests, who frequent the lounge. The group in the lounge, the men, the other guests, seems to increase every night. More and more men meet in the lounge after dinner. They listen to the General's stories. They, the men, the other guests, will, eventually, number hundreds, maybe even thousands. And one day the lounge will not be able to hold them all, and the General will need to speak through a loudspeaker. The General will, indeed, need that type of mechanism, exactly that type of technology, for his jokes and stories and anecdotes to be clearly and distinctly heard. And the meetings after dinner in the lounge will have to be moved outdoors and onto the hotel grounds just to accommodate the cigars, and the smoke from the cigars, cigars by the hundreds, cigars by the thousands, and this will be the time of the neck, of the swollen neck, and of the stiff neck, too, as the other guests, men, attempt to look up, as they strain their necks to see the General, to hear his jokes and stories and anecdotes, to see the way he stands, to study and admire the way he holds his head up, the way he holds his cigar between his fingers. Always conscientious of one another, the other guests, the men, will be helpful, in fact, brotherly, in their way. They will hold each other up, and, if necessary, stand one another on their shoulders, prop one another up, anyway they can.

He is in his room, and it is late at night. It is quite late at night and he is alone, or not alone, in his room. The front desk has already called twice. It is evidently important for him to get the message. There have been many messages left for him. Someone, some party, has been trying to get in touch with him for some time now, incessant telephone calls, and many messages left at his room, slid under his door.

9

It was cool in the summer, even if wasn't supposed to be. A freshness in the air, and that was something entirely new. There were friends, the thought of friends, and still, there was the feeling that there was, somehow, something new. Good things were on the horizon, and, indeed, there was a newness in the air that was, at times, exhilarating. It was the height of the social season, and many other guests were at the hotel at that time. There were weddings, and wedding parties, and certain sections of the hotel were cordoned off. There was much going on. And in the halls, sometimes, he felt like dancing. He felt like he could run and jump, hold his hands out, flex his fingers. It was always that way. And he thought about how he had just begun to relax. The ways in which he had just begun to relax. But the noise was tremendous at that time of year. Still, it was a season, a particular season, and things had to be uniform during that season. Things had to be done in particular and uniform ways, yet there was no telling why. Why? Why, it's a regular party here. Why, I remember one time when I was young. Why, I remember when people, and people were much different then, when people would simply step aside.

There is much to decide during these final days. And maybe he would be better off someplace else. Maybe he would be better off if he just up and left the hotel, didn't even bother to pack his bags. Could you imagine? Just because, and there is no privacy in the world and things get done anyway. And he may end up living in the hotel, if he's not careful, a sort of permanent assignment, or vacation, if you will. But soon after, the conversations in the lounge cease to be about nothing, they cease to be completely superficial, after a time, and eventually turn to more serious subjects. There is the war to discuss, and there are legal proceedings to analyze, always plenty of legal proceedings to analyze, and, by the end of the evening, even the most innocent seeming comments begin to have an uncomfortable edge to them. Still, the hotel is not at all a bad place, he feels. The hotel is, for example, a great place to make connections, a terrific place for meeting the right kind of people. The hotel is, in fact, not a bad place in many ways. It is a fine hotel, a famous hotel, a place for people to come to cure what ails them, a place for people to come when they want to get away from it all.

———

It was time to move forward. A new season had arrived. And, then, there were various attempts made to reach out to others, and there was ample wildlife, game. A whole season's worth of suffering to put behind him, if only he could. It is time to put on your hunting gear. It is time to summon your courage and exercise your best social skills and prove yourself, prove who you are and what you are made of. Perseverance and strength and being polite and being quiet, those and all of the other characteristics that constitute specific personalities, that allow them to succeed. So what if there is no reason, and so what if there is no specific goal or incentive or risk or danger or anything else, apparent or not, there is still quality to rely upon, the quality, the feel, that a person exudes, brings forth, even without trying, and that's what ultimately renders the meaning, that's what fills in the big picture, or allows the big picture to be filled. A gift. A fine gift. Gloves, perhaps. Or a coat. A colorful coat. And the silhouette is unique. And all the animals, even the animals, would, most likely, agree, if they had a say in the matter, if one could actually understand what they said. Indeed, the cats purr, on occasion, when it is warranted, when the desire, or the necessity, is there, he feels. The cats occasionally do wander the halls of the hotel, but mostly they stay put, mostly they stay within their domain, but one does see them, one does, from time to time, hear them, and one does continually feel their presence. It is illuminating at the hotel on that afternoon, he feels, or, rather, it has been a most illuminating day, in general.

There are no secrets among the men, the other guests, in the lounge. However, the conversation is fierce, or, rather, tense, as it is prone to be during those days. Yet, the tone is, more or less, friendly, and the dinner that has preceded the conversation was, as usual, excellent. There are chairs in the lounge as well as ashtrays and fireplaces. It is a grand yet somber place. There are hunting prints, and maps, on the walls. And a great painting and lesser paintings. And the other guests stand and some of them sit as they talk and listen to one another in the dining room and in the lounge. Indeed, there is a great deal of listening required at each evening session.

But he approaches things in the wrong way, he feels. And, in fact, his face has begun to worry him. And his hands. The marks. A preponderance of marks, or signs, that seem to have only recently appeared. And these marks, or signs, bother him. He does not see how the time has passed so quickly. It is as if he has been at the hotel forever, as if his whole life has been spent at a hotel, and this thought, too, bothers him. And as the evening settles in, and as he flicks the ashes from his cigar into a fine standing ashtray, and listens, the thought occurs to him. And it is this thought that urges him, for the first time, to leave the proceedings in the lounge early. It is this thought that urges him up the stairs and down the hall and into his room. He is in his room in the early evening and the noise, its character, is appreciably different. In fact, on that night, his perception of the noise in the lounge is appreciably different. However, there is still much more that needs to be done, and much, in general, to think about. And how fast the time goes. How fast the time goes by. How quickly it all slips by, he feels.

———

And just as he is about to relax, just as he has found the right position to relax in, he remembers something, something he'd meant to say. There was something missing, or something had gone wrong. He was alone in the hotel, in his room, and the night was dark. The hotel was very large and very exclusive, in its way. He is alone in his room when the world begins to shake. He is alone in his room when the world ends, or when it begins to end. He is alone when things begin to crumble, and then there are other matters to consider as well. There is, in fact, a time and place for everything, he feels. He is alone in his room and beginning to relax and it is as if he is standing on a field in the fresh air. The air is fresh on the field, and there is something else, some voice, or some virtue, something special in the way his eyes begin to close. His eyelids are very heavy, at that point. And he really has to do something else, he feels, find some other line of work, but it is the persistence of his dreams, daydreams, this time, that stops him. He is in his room and beginning to relax. There is a hand out. There is definitely something there to consider, but it is not exactly clear what this could possibly be. And there is a reason for this, of course. And it is important to consider what this reason might be, he feels. There is, at first, shining voices, a golden moment, and then something else, some occurrence, or some thought of the future. And this thought, or feeling, is present in his voice, barely audible in his voice, when he talks to himself in his room. He is alone in his room and convinced that something is coming, that some new way of looking at the world is just on the horizon. And time. Time, he feels, at that point, moves very quickly.

10

So it was, as it was, in the first place, a feeling of despair as the band played dinner music in the dining room. He looked around and saw that he was alone. And, at that point, there was no one at the table in the dining room that he recognized. The lessons he'd learned from being alone in a hotel were one and the same, were always one and the same. And so it went on, this existence of his. In a hotel. And on the grass and on the paths and on the dirt roads. Something new each day. But not a home at all. It was always the same, one and the same, the running out of energy as he was about to climb a hill. The doubt as he was about to climb a hill. And trying to take time out of his busy schedule to see the sights, the beautiful mountain vistas and meadows, the beautiful lakes and rivers and streams that provided a very specific backdrop for the hotel. It was one night, and he was sitting on his bed. There was music, popular music, playing, coming from somewhere, maybe from the grounds, or maybe from another guest's room, he couldn't be certain where the music was coming from, but trying to place the music, and before long it started to rain.

It was nighttime. There was the sound of rain on the roof. The weather had been difficult for days. He stood near the entrance to the bar and looked at the hotel lobby. And even on this day, and even in this weather, the guests continue to arrive in a never-ending stream. And if only there had been a library or some other place to go, something nearby, then, maybe, things would have been different. It wasn't so different, though, of course. He had no one nearby. He hadn't a contact for miles. And if he'd run into trouble, he would have had no one to turn to. He'd been alone in the hotel for a long time. And at the back of the bar, set off to one side, there was something unusual, a glass, or a shard of glass, or maybe a light, or something else sharp, he couldn't tell what it was, but it was something, and something he definitely hadn't noticed before. He moved closer to the bar. Maybe he would sit at the bar and order a drink. His stomach was full. He was tired. He hadn't noticed how tired he'd become. And then, all at once, everything changed. He sat at the bar. It was raining. The weather had been bad for weeks. He sat and tried to guess how long the weather had been bad. And at the end of the bar, or behind the bar, a particular glass or bottle, a reflection, or a light, or a quality of light, or something else. He wasn't sure what it was. Perhaps it was something sharp. Still, whatever it was, whatever was there at the end of the bar, or behind the bar, was something, obviously, not to be trifled with.

Not a flame, not an electric bulb, not anything he could quite call out to, not anything he could name, but there was something there, nonetheless, and it was not something new. Something had been there, of course, had been there for as long as he could remember. Like there was morning. It was in the dark. He was still in the dark. He was still in the dark about a lot of things. It seemed that there was supposed to have been quite a few things that he knew about. In fact, he should have known all about what he was supposed to know about. That was kind of obvious. A person is expected to know about things. Still, at that point, there was no one around who was going to test or care or want to find out about what he did or didn't know. He held his hands out, flexed his fingers. The mountain paths were shining, shimmering in the sun, and, in fact, they looked very beautiful and, rather, inviting in the morning light.

The other guests continued to arrive at the hotel, even in the rain. He stood and watched as the other guests continued to arrive at the hotel in a never-ending stream. With a drink in his hand. This, however, required thought, or rather, a certain consideration. And there were walls, and there were doors, and there were locked garden gates, and all of that had to be considered as well. The movement of his body, and the spaces he moved through. The spaces he lived in. And all of that was important, too. It was cold. He was going to go to bed. He had to find his way out of there and to the stairs, and then to his room, and he couldn't risk being seen. It was curious, and it was strange. The hotel. The old hotel. All the same, there were no pictures, or paintings, on the walls, but, all the same, one could feel the presence of pictures, or paintings, on the walls, at all times. The air smelled good in a way he hadn't noticed before. And there were great things to report. And if only he could tell someone about them, and if only there were someone else he could confide in. It was a beautiful spring day, and if only he didn't have to wait, but, that, of course, didn't seem possible. He lived in a room in a hotel. And there were other guests in and around the hotel grounds. But he had to find his way up the stairs, and he couldn't risk being seen. It was important to remember why he was there. At some point, he would certainly have to take a moment out to try and make the pieces of the puzzle fit, so to speak. Perhaps if he spent more time in his room. Perhaps if he declined an invitation or two to the lounge. And his posture was bad. And his thinking was unclear. And there had to be a change, but then, he knew a great change was coming. In fact, change was just around the corner. His head hurt. His feet and legs felt as if they could no longer carry his weight. He was exhausted from the mountain life. Perhaps the mountain air, the mountain life, had, in fact, gotten the best of him. He wasn't sure. However, there were other things, important things, that he had to consider. He was in the garden and he thought that he'd like to pick a flower. And it is beautiful in the garden at that time of day.

11

The key is out of his pocket, in his hand, and he is beginning to wonder why he is still where he is, in the same position. At home. Still in the same position. When he first noticed the mark on his face, on his face over his left eye, specifically. It was cold that morning, and he took a walk. It was one more day, and there was nothing left to do. He couldn't go out. He'd walked all the day before. He was angry and exhausted. There was someone, something, at the end of the hall. Another guest, perhaps, at the end of the hall. And the rest was about enjoyment, and the rest was about a certain kind of suffering. Or, it didn't matter, and no one could tell him that it did. And the mountains looked beautiful from his bedroom window.

There was carpet in the hall and carpet in his room. There was no carpet in the closets. There was carpet in the bar and carpet in the lounge. There was carpet in the lobby and carpet in the dining room. One time, another guest had approached him, had asked him to dance.

There is pouring rain, or, rather, it is pouring rain outside. There are politics in the air that night, on that night, at that time, generally, politics in the air, during that period. There is going to be a change. A great change is already taking place, yet there are very few people who seem to notice. Still, it may be better that way, he feels. It may, in fact, be better, he feels, but, still, there are perhaps even better ways of doing what needs to be done. There are even better ways. And he is able to think about the possibility of better and even better ways of doing things for hours while he is alone in his room. He thinks about politics, the general politics of specific situations, and he thinks about how polite he's been all the while, how polite he's been to the other guests and staff during his stay at the hotel. There is a star in the sky. There are prints and pictures, or, rather, paintings, on the walls of his bedroom and on the walls of the lounge. He enjoys his walks in the forest, his walks along the mountain paths, especially his walks along the mountain paths. The mountain air is, indeed, invigorating. And, on that night, he is thinking of some way of telling the world what it knows, or rather, what it needs to know, some new and better way of telling the world what it needs to know, then, at that point.

———

He sat on a bench in the garden. He'd had many friends when he was younger. He told this to himself often, how he'd had many friends when he was younger, how he'd once been popular and young and had felt more free. It was, of course, a long time ago now. There were no dinners to attend then, and not very many social calls or visits. Some of the other guests would bring their pets into the dining room, and into the lounge, before and after dinner. The mountain air was uncommonly good for his complexion, just like it was for a lot of other people. And, in fact, he wasn't so different from other people, after all. In fact, he thought he had a lot in common with other people. After all, he'd had friends, and his friends had been good and strong and right a lot of the time, right in the things they'd said, right in their conclusions.

———

There were a hundred of them there, at least a hundred honored guests, and there were bonfires and there was food and there was much, at that time, to marvel at. A holiday had come. There were many festivities, and nothing could spoil the enjoyable atmosphere.

And if only he'd been an industrialist, a politician, a clergyman, a hunter, a soldier, an assassin, a lover, a spy, or anything at all.

He could hear people coughing and crying and asking for help. There was a burning smell, an aroma, or odor, the scent of something burning in the air. The scent of something burning, and if anyone would have cared to listen. He could have heard voices, and it was curious the way the world ended, the way things ended, so suddenly, after all. And soon it would be done, the suffering would be done too. And he would have no need for exercise, or worry, or for anything at all. It was on par with the way the world already was, the way he'd always believed the world to be. There was no need to suffer. There was no need to think the way he sometimes thought. His way of thinking was, after all, often unhealthy and unwise. It was safer to sit off in the distance, it was healthier to mix with people, it was healthier to do what was asked of him, what was expected of him. It was safer to dream. And to dream. He was awake. Life in the hotel, his life, was slow, so slow, sometimes, it never seemed to end.

The hotel was in the mountains, high enough, famously, to inspire one toward a contemplative type of existence. The rooms were large and comfortable. He would meet people. He was sure he would make at least one important and lasting contact during his stay at the hotel.

The road led to the right, and then it turned sharply to the left. There were very few cars on the road, at that point, but there must have been something there, if not another car, then perhaps it had been an animal after all. He'd heard a dull sound, felt something against the front of the car, and then the wheel slipped. It was horrible to lose control. It was horrible to lose control in that way. And while he was spinning. And while he was out of control. No. Think. There was someone above him. He had been going out of town. He had been sent to attend a dinner, or to receive a message, an award, or he had been carrying out some other important assignment, a kind of vacation. He was sure he was good at his job. He'd done everything that was asked of him. Still, he had no close friends. He ate his lunch alone. He would often sit on park benches and eat his lunch alone. But now, finally, he was making progress. He wasn't even particularly comfortable in the situation, the position, he found himself in, and still he was making progress, good progress. The countryside, the area surrounding the hotel, was legendary for its beauty, for its curative powers. Indeed there was much to learn about the customs and culture of the people who lived, who spent all of their time in the area that surrounded the hotel. He was sure, so sure, of what he wanted. It was right, and there was no reason to think otherwise, and there was certainly no reason to explode. Don't explode. He was in love. No, he wasn't in love. He'd had an understanding, but not really that either. Things changed. He knew that things changed. It was the best that could be said. And he'd repeated the best that could be said many, many times before, and in exactly the right ways, too. Again. And no one had asked him to do what he'd been told to do. There was progress, however, real progress was being made. It was in the sunshine one afternoon. He was sitting in the sunshine and thinking, or not merely thinking. He was doing something about his problems. And at the edge of the road, off to the side, for just a second, he thought he might have seen an animal. It had to have been an animal. It couldn't have been anything else. But of all the people in the world, to see an animal there at that time, in that position.

He was sitting at the bar and watching the scene in the hotel lobby. Other guests were continuing to arrive in a never-ending stream. And it was curious, the way the other guests arrived, how they continued to arrive by car. He didn't even own a car, had never even owned a car. It was, however, exciting in those days. And sometimes there were invitations, and then the invitations would be forgotten. But what of that? He was not one to make a fuss. He was, typically, not even one to notice. And then there was something moving at the edge of the woods. The road ran through a large forest. There was something moving, something that wasn't already dead. The car was wrecked. He was alone. Something bad had happened to the driver. And, all along, he'd wanted to thank the driver. The world was a big place. Telling them. He was telling them something, and then he'd stopped, had stopped himself, from telling them something. He'd been driving the car, had been driving a car, had been driven in a car. There was a driver. There had been a driver. And then there was something there, something right in front of him on the road, right in front of the car. And, sometimes, he'd forget. In front of him. Sometimes, he'd forget. He looked out the window. The rearview mirror was behind the bar. And it was clear that this was something, an observation, an impression, an object, perhaps, to be maintained. Indeed, whatever was behind the bar was definitely something not to be trifled with. And it was dangerous to drive in the country, on country roads, on forest roads, in the mountains, at night. Everyone had always told him so.

He sat on a bench in the garden. There were other guests in the garden that day. It was a windy day, and he felt a bit tired. This, of course, could not be avoided. Feeling tired, now and again, could not be avoided, mainly because of his condition, his serious condition.

12

It was hard for one to understand. It was hard for anyone to get inside. The gate was fantastically strong, well constructed. He put his shoulder into it. He lifted, pushed, pulled at the gate, and still it wouldn't budge. There was a difference, though, this time. He had evidently overstepped his bounds. And what a place it was. He was determined to succeed. And in the last place he'd ever expected to find himself. It was one way or the other, always one way or the other. A personal challenge, a vacation, or an assignment, or a specific task, a job, that had to be accomplished, and had to be accomplished soon, by the last day of the week, if possible. It was the last day of the week, and he had to find a way to unlock the gate. The gate was locked, and it was, he believed, the last place on the hotel grounds he had not visited, had not stepped inside. Indeed, it appeared as if the gate were rarely, if ever, opened. And it was exciting, certainly exciting, at that point, to try something new.

There were plants, mostly ivy. And he had to find a way inside. In the morning he'd looked around. He'd looked out the window of his room and had discovered the secret that had eluded him for a very long time. And it was great to be in a position of discovery, in a position of personal triumph, in the right position, in the position he'd always wanted to be in. But, by then, of course, things were different. There was work to be done. He'd sat in his room and waited. He'd waited and waited. He'd attended enough dinners and social functions to know. And it was with a sense of purpose that he approached the gate. He would remember the way it was done this time. The ground was wet. He had no time left to fool around. He had no time left to wander. It was towards the end of his stay at the hotel. Close. There was something, just around the corner. There was something, someone, in his room. A deep and impossible mystery, a secret. And on the grounds, all around the hotel grounds, and at that point, and at that time. Do you come here often? Have you stayed here before? Have you been here long? How long are you planning to stay? Is there someone, something, else, Sir? Someone, something, else, I can help you find?

———

The gate was long and tall and made of wrought iron. The gate was decorated with intricate patterns: snakes or deer or bears. It was hard to tell what the design was, what the pattern was supposed to represent. In the morning he woke up and asked himself a question, a whole series of questions. There was, of course, a way into the garden. The garden was impossible to see, impossible to recognize from the outside. There was no way in. He'd checked along the sides and around the back many, many times, but there was no way in. He needed a ladder, a length of rope. And, at one point, he'd been asleep in his car.

———

He shook the gate, and as he shook the gate, his excitement increased. This was something new. He was going to enter the garden. He was going to see what was inside. He was a, more or less, private person. He'd lived a quiet life. And, still, it was surprising, sometimes surprising, when he found himself in such a situation, in such a position, well positioned, so to speak, for opportunity. It was most surprising and most disquieting, too, in its way. And, at times, it was like a dream, like a real dream, in fact, just like the dream he'd had.

———

There was not a moment to spare, he had to get inside the garden, open the garden gate. His curiosity was overwhelming. And as each day went by, it had gotten a little worse. It broke his heart. He had to consider himself unlucky. And in the long run he had been unlucky. One of the unluckiest of all. There had been dogs howling all night. A great hunt was set to take place that very morning. A hunting party had been assembled. A great group of men, other guests, with weapons and dogs and horses. They, the other guests, set off early one morning. There was no denying that they, the other guests, appeared to be a strong and robust group. They looked powerful and handsome as they set off early one morning for a hunt. But the dogs, the hunting dogs, had kept him up all night. Still, there was no denying the positive impression the other guests gave, seemed to have about them, as they rode into the forest on their horses with the hunting dogs at their sides. And as hard as it was to understand. It was hard to understand exactly why that gate and that garden, specifically, had been closed, had been hidden from view in the first place. There was no sign on the gate, conspicuously no law, nor rule, nor prohibition posted anywhere. Indeed, there was no apparent reason for him, nor for anyone else, to not be allowed to enter. But if he hadn't been invited to participate in the hunt, or, rather, if he had been invited to participate in the hunt. If only he'd been invited to participate in the hunt.

The gate was old. It was covered with ivy and branches. An ornamental gate, decorated with intricate patterns: snakes or deer or bears, he couldn't tell which. He couldn't tell what the pattern was supposed to represent. And it, the gate, must have been beautiful at one time. He couldn't help feeling, though, that it had taken him an inordinately long time to discover this place, and the hidden treasure, the treasure that must have been hidden deep inside the garden. And it hadn't been that long. It hadn't, in fact, been that long ago. And there must be some good reason to go on, to continue, he feels. But the weather was bad. It had rained for days. Days and days of rain. And still there was no sign of life in the garden from what little he could see from where he was standing outside the gate. The rest of his morning was spent relaxing. He took a seat at the bar and ordered a drink. He spent the afternoon at the bar and drank his drink slowly. It was unseasonable weather, yet, at that point, there was no reason to believe that he'd had anything to do with it. Still there was fear. And what if he were to fall or to seriously injure himself while he was climbing the garden gate?

13

The end of the road, or, rather, the end of the path. A face in the woods startled him. It was coming back. He thought of the garden. Of all the afternoons he had spent in the garden. Who he was. It was a face like any other. A harmony of lines, a pleasing silhouette, but he couldn't forget, couldn't quite remember, his reason for being there. His vacation had begun a year ago, or so. His vacation had begun suddenly, and it would soon be over. There was a face by the bushes, near the edge of the path. The face was not unpleasant to look at. By degrees, he had changed. Spending time in the garden had been good. Spending time outdoors had generally been good for him. But in the lounge the night before. There was an important announcement that was about to be made on the radio. And many of the men, other guests, had gathered in the lounge to listen to the radio.

At the edge of the path, just inside the bushes, there was a face. The face was, in fact, quite pleasing to look at. A year ago, just about a year ago, or so. He had been driving the car. The driver had been whistling the tune to a popular song. The car radio was on. An animal was in the middle of the road. Or there was a stop, or there was some reason the car had stopped. There had been a violent collision. He had been thrown forward in his seat. He had seen the animal's eyes. He had seen an animal, or something else still alive, stare at him from the bushes. It was a pleasant afternoon. The summer had been most pleasant and mild. Many of the other guests had remarked upon the unseasonably mild weather. Yes, there was a certain amount of disappointment, here and there, but, for the most part, the other guests seemed pleased, surprised and pleased, with the weather, with the way things were. And one must maintain a positive attitude throughout. And there is no telling exactly why he found the face so pleasing. Perhaps it was the lines, the delicate shadow, the mystery of its silhouette. There was a reason for his having gone out that night, though. He'd left his room, or he'd left home. He had been unhappy. But the trees calmed him. The mountain air was special, and after days and weeks and months of exercise and eating well, his appearance changed. He could see his face reflected in the mirror that hung behind the bar.

Something in the woods stared back at him. He stepped back, and was afraid, afraid, but excited. He'd been at the hotel for an entire season. The other guests were, mostly, fine. Most of them, the other guests, were very nice, and he'd rather enjoyed being in their company. He'd enjoyed the long walks he'd taken around the hotel grounds. And once there had been a fire, a great fire. Now, however, there was no evidence of fire. He stood in front of the great gates of the locked garden and wondered how he would ever get inside. There was a face in the bushes, maybe a face, or possibly shadows, shadows cast from the afternoon sun. Whichever way it was, whatever it was that was staring at him, or not staring at him, the sensation of being stared at was not, at that point, in the least bit unpleasant. And, in the end, there was not that much to worry about. There was a lot to see around the hotel grounds, there was much to remark upon, and, in the end, isn't that exactly what he'd come there for?

There was something in the middle of the path. There was a face in the bushes. He'd tried to find his way into the garden. He'd searched and searched and had tried hard to find a door, an entrance of some kind. And there had to be a way in. The wrought iron gates were beautiful in the sun, decorated as they were with intricate patterns: snakes, or bears, or deer. He couldn't tell what the pattern was supposed to represent. It was hard to imagine. A beautiful afternoon. And if he closed his eyes. Imagine a fire. He could, almost, smell something, an odor, or an aroma, of some kind, coming from inside the gate.

It was almost time to eat. His current schedule was heavily regulated by food, by mealtimes. He sat on a bench on a path, one of the many paths that formed intricate patterns over and around the hotel grounds. He enjoyed the afternoon sun. Imagine a fire, though. What the scene must have looked like.

And he'd stumbled out onto the road. The eyes were staring back at him. He could see that the animal was injured, would have been badly injured. The car was only a short distance from a field. He would go to the field and ask for help. There had to be someone who lived nearby, someone whom he could ask for help.

It was a starless night. On the road. The car's headlights were still on. It was very quiet. There was a face in the bushes by the bench where he sat. The face was pleasant to look at. Its outline, its shadow, its delicate silhouette. There was red on the wall. The wall was painted red. The path turned slightly, and then turned abruptly, as it wound around the side of the mountain, and then there were the views of the hotel from various vantage points on the path as well. The city was beautiful, too, sometimes, for what it was worth, even he could see that. A beautiful hotel set high in the mountains, surrounded by a great wrought iron fence. The magnificence of the hotel was a sight to behold. And there was honor in being invited, in one's being invited, to the hotel. But the halls are never quiet, and there is always the noise of the lamps, of the lights, of electricity. The lights in the hall are never turned off. And he could see a star, one, at first, and then more and more, from where he was standing near the window in his room.

———

It was the middle of summer. He had to begin heading back. He'd eaten a late lunch outdoors and had returned to the car feeling well. And, indeed, there was something startling about his being in the car again. Its noise, the car's noise, was jarring. He started the engine. He still had a long drive ahead of him. It would soon be dark. The road led through the forest. In fact, he had not been worried at all. Still, he would have to stop somewhere for the night. Time moved forward, or the time moved very slowly. It was a night like many other nights, except that on this night there was an important announcement that was supposed to be made on the radio.

———

The men, the other guests in the lounge, were gathered around the radio. The other guests listened to the announcement in silence. It was after dinner. Some of the men were smoking cigars. The General was smoking a cigar. And each one of them, the other guests, in turn, reacted in some appreciable way, and he noted, or rather, he was in a position to note, their reactions.

———

It was a silent face, a beautiful, sad, and silent face. The face was pleasant to look at and he wanted very much to be able to see it. He stared at the face out of the corner of his eye. A marvelous sort of face. And, really, a face anyone would have wanted to look at. But in the back of his mind, if he thought about it at all clearly, he was sure that the car had hit an animal. There had been a sound, a dull thud at first, and then a louder sound, maybe a sharp crack. The car had hit something. It couldn't have continued anyway, he knew that. Even the driver had said so. But he'd wanted it to continue. He'd wanted everything to stay the same. They had been expecting him. It was important, the timing of his arrival was important. But now, and the world waits for no man, he feels.

14

It was early, then. His waking up was, however, something special. And there was a reserve in his step, a sort of, more or less, positive attitude about him, in the way he carried himself. Indeed, he walked as if he were a man with nothing on his mind, no cares, no worries. The halls were well lit that morning, as well lit as they usually were, or so it seemed to him. He held his hands out, flexed his fingers. There were the usual nods to the other guests and staff he passed by. And there was smoke in the air. A cigarette left smoldering in an ashtray. And the thought that concerned him, at that point, had to do with water, something about water, and, of course, with the way other people thought about him. He worried about the way others thought about him. It was not unusual for him to be up very early in the morning. There were a few guests about, and staff, too. They were helpless, the children were helpless. Were all children helpless? Really helpless without their mothers and fathers? He would see them in the morning, sometimes, running around, children, other guests, orphans almost, without activities of their own. It was the morning, and he'd woken up with a tremendous amount of energy. He'd dressed and had left his room thinking all kinds of thoughts. And there was no going back to his room. Still, he couldn't quite get himself to leave his room in exactly the right way, at exactly the right time. He'd wanted. He would have to listen, however. He would have to listen to his own body very carefully if he was going to continue to wake up at the right time.

The plants that grew along the garden path were green. The path was wet from the rain. He walked slowly down the garden path and tried to gather as much of the warm sunlight into him, into his body, as he could. In the morning light, the path was most beautiful, was at its most beautiful. There were branches and leaves and ivy and vines of every kind, and on that morning, everything was very green. He walked and held his head up straight, he put his hands out, flexed his fingers.

———

His signal had arrived the night before. It had arrived abruptly. It was not the type of signal he had been expecting, though. Still, he had hoped that night, the way he'd always hoped at night, for some word to arrive out of the blue and bring him good news, unexpected good news. And when his signal had actually arrived, he'd felt an odd excitement, or, rather, a strong anticipation about things that he had not ever felt before, at least not quite in that way.

———

There were people about, people, in general, who, it seemed, had something to do. He would see them, these other guests, once in a while. He would see them pass and then not see them again for some time. And what a dream it was to be in such a position. And indeed, his position could only inspire the most hopeful kinds of thoughts.

———

They were selling fruit, or at least he thought it was fruit, on the mountain path. The mountain path was beautiful, yet the selling of fruit, the fact of it, made no sense, and, in fact, there was no reason for him to buy fruit. There was really no reason for him to have even thought about fruit, at that point. Still, there was a kind of envy in the way he looked at the man selling the fruit, the fruit seller, and his boxes, the way the boxes were set along the mountain path. And there was no denying that he was hungry. There was no denying that he needed to get something to eat, but the thought of the fruit seller made him feel, somehow, sick, or rather, nauseated. It may have been that he had not noticed this fruit seller before, or it may have been because he was hungry. There was an unwarranted accusation made, or there was a commotion of some sort, or there was a dispute about something, that made him move his chair back and stand up from the dining room table. There were several of them, men, mostly, other guests, who'd moved their chairs back and stood up and looked toward the table where the trouble was. He stood up and then walked out of the room, or out of the hotel. It was nerve-wracking, there had been some trouble, a commotion of some sort, and he'd had a bad dream, but he'd woken up with a tremendous amount of energy, an uncharacteristic amount of energy, that morning.

He thought of nothing in particular as he walked down the mountain path. And there was something missing from his room. It seemed like he'd been at the hotel for a long time. He'd wanted to take something home, towels, a couple of washcloths, an ashtray, a box of matches, something with the hotel's name on it, a souvenir of his stay, of sorts. And there had to be something. But there was never the right opportunity. He was always too busy. He could have walked to the village. He knew the way to the village, of course, but it was not a walk that he thought he'd like to make, not at that point. There had been no reason for him to go to the village. The mountain air was particularly invigorating in the morning. It smelled especially clean and fresh and good right after the sun had risen. And, in the end, his taking a walk in the morning had turned out to have been the right decision.

When the program ended, or when the program resumed, after the announcement had been made on the radio, he'd felt relieved. There was no sense of betrayal, nothing that could have made him feel responsible in anyway. But some of the men, the other guests, had seemed bothered, had seemed a bit agitated, even frightened, in a way. There had been a good deal of talk, of conversation, afterwards. And the conversation had had an unexpected effect on him. In fact, it had been an agony of sorts for him to have had to sit in silence. Still, there had been some measure of virtue, at that point, in his having successfully sat and said nothing. And he had been virtuous. He had spent time among them, the other guests, and, on more than one occasion, had not said a single word.

15

Boiling over for really no reason at all. It could have been a life, a full life, a life filled with profundities, but instead it was, he guessed, it was to be, in fact, a life filled with humiliations, little humiliations, and, what was more, humiliations without cause. The other guests stared at him blankly. He hadn't said a word, and still they stared. It was humiliating to be in such a state, in such a position. And then there were the sounds. Sounds suspended in the air, and vacant, and there might have been more, observations, positive ways of looking into and at the situation, his position. His job and the mountain life, in general, had made him very tired. And there was glass, broken pieces of glass, tiny broken pieces of glass on the walkway, the path, really. And there was no one else around. There must have been a party, however, a drinking party, perhaps, the night before.

He imagined the two of them talking, or a whole party of people talking. And the hotel. And how pathetic to be a ghost. And those people, the other guests, the staff, the occasional people from the village, they were worse than enemies, they were worse than strangers. He'd see them every day. He'd see them in the halls and on his walks. He'd see them and talk to them, and every one of them in their fine clothes and with their blank stares, and each one of them so serious about their holidays and their vacations and their seasons away from it all. Still, there was much to be grateful for, and there was much to be relieved, even happy, about. Strange thoughts entered his head, specific daydreams about strangers, famous figures, who would sometimes come to help him.

There was a sound from outside his window. He regularly left the window in his room open, just slightly, to let in the air. And then there was a sound, a clinking, or tinkling, a jangling sound, really, someone walking a pet, perhaps the sound of a pet's collar, someone taking a pet out for air? He'd seen the villagers walking goats and sheep and cows on and around the mountain paths, when he'd ventured that far. The hotel was very large. It was, in fact, a massive and imposing structure. There were no two ways about it, the hotel was grand, and the old hotel had been even grander still, in its day. And there was the garden gate to consider as well. The wrought iron gate with its intricate pattern: snakes, or bears, or deer. He couldn't tell exactly what was supposed to have been represented by the pattern, by its design. But he was sure that the gate held mysteries deep inside.

Once it was not like this. At one time it was different. Once mountains were greater than people. There was a certain respect. He was sure about a lot of things, then. He knew where he was going when he left home. He knew who he was. There were clowns in the circus and magicians in the theaters up and down the boulevard, and street life, and characters he knew well, but that was only one dimension of his existence. A single dimension. A singular aspect. And if it had been what it was supposed to have been, what he'd supposed it had been, then even the surprises, the unexpected occurrences, would not have hurt him. But this being what it was. This being exactly what it was, and what it was, exactly, in spite of itself.

There was the thought of this thing and of that thing. He had to bend down, stoop, to pick up the pieces of glass, examine them, hold the small pieces in his hands. He had to bend down, stoop, to pick up a handful of leaves. His purpose. His reason for being there. He could almost imagine being inside the garden now. How it must have looked. Perhaps the locked garden looked a little like the garden he was sitting in now?

He must have looked. He could have recovered. There was a day once. A special day. And within the special day, a golden moment. He had come to the hotel in haste. He had spent all of his time there rushing around. He had first done this thing and then that thing. He had not relaxed, and, in the end, the hotel had not brought him enjoyment or rest or new contacts. In fact, the whole experience had been something of a waste of time, and now his stay was almost over. He no longer felt like a guest, would soon no longer be a guest. And that burning desire to rush. It was all along the gate. The gate was tall, and it was impossible to climb. It was overgrown, overrun, with weeds and ivy and branches. It was easy to miss.

There must have been a mistake. There couldn't have been an animal involved at all. Not an animal. And the eyes he'd seen from the bushes. The eyes had to have been, well, he wasn't sure what, but the sound. The sound, a thump, or a crack, or whatever it was, whatever it had sounded like, had been sickening to hear, had, in the end, nauseated him, made him sick, in a way.

He had to get up. He had to go somewhere. And when he put his hands out, flexed his fingers, he could almost touch a tree, a tree with branches that hung very low over the gate. There was something in the General's eye. The General took out a handkerchief and began rubbing his eye, but still continued to talk. He had continued to talk, and all the while he rubbed his eye with a handkerchief. It was long ago, the General said, the story's events had taken place a long time ago. So much of it had been forgotten, but, then, who could forget such a thing? And who would think such things in the first place? It wasn't like he'd been forced to drive, to accept a ride, to climb up a hill. No one, in fact, had held a gun to his head. It wasn't that way at all. He'd had plenty to live for. He was a happy man. And there were people. Yes, there were people he loved. Loved, honored, cherished.

———

But the deer. It wasn't a deer, was it? It couldn't have been a deer. He would have known immediately if it had been a deer. He'd seen deer, of course, could recognize a deer. But it had been an animal, a heavy animal, and the car had stopped moving. And he'd managed to get out of the car and walk to the side of the road.

———

It was late one night and he was driving through the forest. He was on assignment for his job. He was going on vacation, and he was driving through the forest, on a forest road. The forest was mysterious. And there were animals that lived in the forest. It was a forest, like any other forest, and it was full of animals of all kinds. It was a starless night and then there was a sound, dull at first, and then louder, sharp, a thud, or a thump, or a crack. And if truth be told. For the world outside. The incident was difficult, was made even more complicated by the fact that whatever it was, whichever kind of animal it had been, had eyes, had had large eyes, and he had seen these eyes off to the side of the road. He had seen these eyes, these hurt eyes, and then they had gone, disappeared, just like that, in an instant, disappeared into the forest.

———

It was an end, of course, a type of end. The end of his vacation. He had been on vacation for a long time. And, in the future, when they asked him about his vacation, he would inevitably smile. He would say a word or two, and then the conversation would continue without him. It would be as easy as that. It would be easy to do that, in just that way. And there would be the feeling of his having shared something. Something would have been shared. But the mountain air, and the air, in general, at that particular time of year. There was no sense of panic, not yet, not then, not at that point. He hadn't even packed his bags because it was not time for that either. Indeed, there was still time. Dependable time. Or, rather, time he could depend on.

16

There was a cause for it all, of course. The moaning, or groaning, and crying and screaming at night. Someone, something, had woken up. There was a split in the night. He was trying to sleep. He had been very tired, exhausted, really, and there was no telling, would be no telling, anyone, anything. A day to get out and take a drive. Drive the car. The car on the street. All his bags were neatly packed. He would get in the car and drive himself. The forest was beautiful at night. He was, however, put off by the way the staff spoke to him. He was put off and, somewhat, frightened at the same time. He was sure there was something in the bushes. And if he rolled the window down, the car window, he knew he would hear their voices on the wind. He was sure their voices would carry all the way up to his room, through the open window, and into his room.

The air was dry. It was an unusually warm and dry evening. The only warm day since he'd arrived at the hotel. And the way the time moved, or didn't move, worried and, somewhat, frightened him. He could have driven a car, maybe he should have driven the car, but, then, if the same thing would have happened, if he had not been the one to go and get help. It was a warm morning. The air was dry. He had been kept up most of the night before by the sound of the wind and by the sound of a party, or dogs, a wedding party, perhaps. The hotel was an ideal spot for a wedding. And a garden had been cordoned off. An entire area near the bushes had been cordoned off for what appeared to be a party of some sort.

He had observed the other guests as they arrived in a, seemingly, never-ending stream. And now it was time to leave. And if he were to leave the hotel, he could not have imagined a better time for doing it than then, at that point. The mountains, however, were beautiful. And he saw the same people. He heard their voices. Still, there was not much to be said about them. A face while he ate his soup. A question as he was about to excuse himself from the table. A question while he smoked a cigarette at the bar. He was standing by the door of the bar. And isn't it a pity there isn't a casino, or a library, nearby? He approached the door slowly. He was sure that his time and effort had been justified. It was high time to leave, to pack his bags and go. But there is just no reason for that sort of behavior. Silly, really, isn't it? Grown men. It is the surprise of the season, I suppose, but what a way to wreck. Even if it is temporary. Ha! A perfect holiday.

And I always wake up screaming, don't you? I will always remember the screaming. And, if this doesn't bother you? I'm not imposing myself on you, am I? After all, you were there. You remember, don't you?

And the singing. It was a song, a popular song. But, by then, the song had finished. The couple, the other guests, who had been married were young, one could tell by the singing, the songs, the popular songs that were sung at the wedding party.

There was a spirit of compromise in the air. The war had begun. He was sure that the staff was happy to see him go. And the car was waiting, the driver had been waiting for over an hour, and the telephone had rung, and there had been a knock at his door, and then, after a few moments, he remembered the words to a popular song, a song he remembered having heard somewhere at least once before. Yet, to his mind, popular songs were mostly the same. The singing was poor. Still, there was definitely no one else around who would have been able to sing the song any better, or, for that matter, sing the song at all. Once in a while someone would play the piano in the lounge, and the other guests would sing, and he would be obliged to sing as well. A whole country, a whole world, in a way, like a country or a whole world, and there would be knowing smiles, sometimes, and gestures, sometimes, and always lots of laughter. And then the night came and he was sure, certain, that he would be leaving. His signal was waiting for him in his room. Still, there was no telling exactly where the signal had originated from, but it was certainly time to go, high time to go, in a way.

There was the memory, of course, his memory. His capacity for memory was perhaps the most important part of his job, or, rather, his most useful characteristic. A page turning, and he smiled at himself. There were prayers in the hotel chapel, in the smallest of the hotel's many chapels, one of the many convenient, serene, and beautiful sites for worship that the hotel offered its guests. And there were prayers, he could hear prayers, coming from the smallest of the hotel's several chapels. There was a small hotel chapel, a chapel on a hill, a hill that could be clearly and distinctly seen from several vantage points in and around the hotel grounds. He heard prayers from inside the chapel, and he was sure they were prayers, not in any way popular songs, not popular songs, but, in fact, prayers, or rather, hymns. And one has to remember. Consequences. Actions. Remember. Remember why they're here.

He put on his glasses, he hadn't noticed how many people, other guests, wore glasses, how common it was for the people, the other guests, at the dining room table, for example, to be wearing glasses. He had been assigned a specific seat at a specific table in the dining room, and night after night he had had his meals at the same table. There was a wedding at the hotel, a wedding party, and someone had begun singing a song, a popular song, and it was , in fact, a song he'd heard, at least once, one time, before.

———

It was with a real sense of satisfaction. He put out his cigarette. He walked down the hall. The air was still and silent as he got out of the car. It was quiet, but there were sounds, had been sounds, then, he was sure of it, in retrospect. Still, he hadn't noticed. What exactly was it that had bothered him? It was a bother, the singing was a bother, and so was the driving, and the walking, activities, in general, were a bother, the whole idea of a vacation itself was a bother, the very idea that he needed a vacation, that people took vacations. The hotel was an ideal spot for a wedding. But this elicited laughter. He had said something funny, inadvertently, and everyone who'd heard it had laughed. And the laughter surprised him, still, somehow, surprised him. It was something he hadn't noticed, at first, hadn't, at first, quite expected, and there was something else, the question of what exactly had happened, of what his position had been, of what he'd been there for, indeed, the whole question of his purpose. He'd gone for help, was about to go for help. He'd looked away from the road. He'd looked to the side of the road, and he could have sworn he'd seen something, a pair of eyes, that had been deeply wounded, hurt, by something. And then a clearing, a clearing in the forest, or a field, an open space of some kind. He'd gone for help. He'd gone for help, hadn't he? He'd go for help and the driver would live, and the thing in the bushes, the animal, if that's what it was, would escape unharmed. Thank God. But it was never quite clear, not to him, at least, and certainly not then, what it was he'd said that had been so very funny.

Part II - Funeral

1

The funeral ended. It was after the funeral. There were cars parked along the grass, the long expanse of grass. And there was a golden moment. It was just the way it was supposed to be. It was splendid and beautiful. There was even someone. And the grass was green. And there were others there as well. Friends, associates, and relatives, and other people, strangers, if you will. He was handsome, had been even more handsome in life. He was always one for photos, for living, for looking handsome. It could have been a better life, though. He could have had better friends, associates. In short, he could have made better choices.

He was there once. In the middle of the street. On the concrete pedestrian island in the middle of the street. He was waving his hands, gesturing, somewhat wildly, humiliatingly, in a way, doing a kind of dance, almost a dance, trying to catch their attention, his friends, associates, the people he was supposed to be meeting for lunch. It was the middle of the day, in the middle of the city, and there was no one else around. But somehow that's wrong, not exactly right, in fact, not at all the right way to put it. There was a ribbon around his neck, or around her neck. A red bag. Or a green, or red, door. A guitar, perhaps. It wasn't exactly clear.

There was a ribbon around someone's neck. A red bag. Or a green, or red, door. There was supposed to be a meeting for lunch. Not a meeting exactly, just good friends, associates, getting together for lunch. In fact, the food was delicious. The weather in the city had been great. His good friends, associates, sat around the table and talked the way good friends, associates, often do. But there was a kind of pressure in the air. Still, the consensus around the table was that the funeral had been handled expertly, had been handled in an expert manner. The consensus around the table was that the funeral could not have been handled any better. And they'd made a plan to meet that day. His good friends, associates.

———

He was standing in the middle of the street, waving his hands, gesturing, somewhat wildly, humiliatingly, in a way, doing a kind of dance, almost a dance, trying to get their attention, his friends, associates. And he'd called her on the telephone. He'd asked her to come to the café, or restaurant, to meet with him. He'd arranged a meeting. And there was no telling how fast all of this occurred.

———

But there were flowers, real flowers, mostly, and artificial ones, too. There was also a fire that day. A large explosion rocked the city. There were sirens in the distance. There was a major fire somewhere, and tragedy, and difficulties, and suffering, but they'd made a plan to meet for lunch.

———

He stood in the middle of the street and waved his hands, gestured, somewhat wildly, humiliatingly, in a way, did a kind of dance, almost a dance. And there was something slightly pathetic about the way he moved, about what he was trying to accomplish, then, at that point, pathetic, and humiliating, in a way.

———

He stood in the middle of the street and his arms were full. It was winter, and he'd been shopping, doing holiday shopping, and his arms were full of bags and packages. It was cold, and he was wearing a scarf. He'd seen her approach the café door. A red bag. There was a red bag. Or, maybe, a green, or red, door. He'd tried to wave, had tried to get her attention, but he'd dropped what he'd been holding in his arms, bags, packages, perhaps a red bag, or maybe a box, all over the street.

———

The hearse arrived with the casket inside. It parked against the curb. The curb ran alongside a road, ran alongside a large expanse of grass. And there was no telling, then, at that point, just how long the funeral would last.

———

He is eating a sandwich after returning home from work. He is eating a sandwich at home after work, and it is an ordinary evening, or afternoon. He is eating dinner, or lunch, on an otherwise ordinary evening, or afternoon. It is an evening, or afternoon, that could have started, that could not have started, in a more ordinary way. And there is no one on the street, not at that point.

———

It was a beautiful day in the middle of the city.

———

He had gone to get lunch, a sandwich, and had unexpectedly ended up in the exact restaurant, or café, in fact, in the very same restaurant, or café. He had been hoping to meet his friends, associates, or he had been hoping to meet someone else, by surprise, perhaps.

———

The funeral had been a success, was, more or less, successful, in its way. In fact, the funeral had been well planned, well conceived, well thought-out. And many people had attended the funeral, friends, associates, and relatives, and others. There were many people there, in the cemetery, at one time.

2

There was a knock at the door. Yet, he was never really the type to have visitors.

———

And there were friends, associates, and relatives, and others, who'd attended the funeral.

———

He looked around the corner, looked up and down the street. And the night before he had been reluctant to call her on the telephone. There was a tone, a voice, that she sometimes used. And he had been, more or less, reluctant to call her on the telephone.

———

The funeral took place on a Monday.

———

Tuesday was his favorite day of the week, had been his favorite day of the week. Good things often seemed to happen to him on Tuesdays. Yet there was nothing special to do that day, not at that point. And, in fact, it would have been perfectly fine for him not to have called her that day.

———

There were flowers at the funeral. Real flowers, and artificial ones, too. Arrangements of flowers, floral arrangements, really, or bouquets, set along the grass.

It was after the funeral, and his friends, associates, had made a plan, an arrangement. His friends, associates, had planned, arranged, to meet at a café after the funeral.

He was on a train. In the dream he'd had, he was on a train. And it was different then. Before the crisis. Before death. All the death. Before death, or crisis. In the dream he'd had he was at the mercy of strangers. Before death, or crisis. All the death. Or before fortune, if you will, good or bad fortune. Still, it, what was happening to him in his dream, what had already happened to him in his dream, was frightening. There was a wall on the train. There was a wall on the train, a divide, of sorts, very thin, that separated him from the outside. All that stood between him and the outside world, at that point, in his dream, was a, more or less, thin wall on the train. And he could hear things, things moving, on the other side of the wall on the train. And at one time he'd lived in an apartment. And he was sure that his apartment had not been an impressive place. He was sure that there had, in fact, been something missing from his apartment. In the dream he'd had there had been something, something important, missing from his apartment.

There were flowers at the funeral. Real flowers, and artificial ones, too. Arrangements of flowers, floral arrangements, really, or bouquets, set along the grass. And mourners, of course, as well.

The café was like home, sometimes, something like home. Something like a home away from home. Yet he was often not at home, and this fact bothered and, sometimes, frightened him. He'd danced at the café, or restaurant, regularly, at one time, when there'd been music. He'd dance there, at the café, or restaurant, regularly, when there was music. He was going to call her on the telephone, but he was hesitant, more or less, reluctant, if you will. In fact, his apartment was a mess, had been a mess for weeks. It was getting harder and harder to find things. And he could see her through the window. He thought he'd seen her through the café, or restaurant, window. He thought he'd looked up at precisely the right time and had seen her. He was standing in the middle of the street, on the concrete pedestrian traffic island in the middle of the street, and he could see her, and it wasn't at all like a movie or a story in a book. It wasn't at all like anything he could picture, or imagine, beforehand. His apartment was typically very quiet at night. But sometimes, he'd hear noises. The sound, through the wall, or ceiling, of a person moving. It was after work, one day, and he was tired. He sat and stared out the window of the café.

———

And his friends, associates, reached the café in no time. It is, in fact, a short distance, a pleasant walk, on most days, from the cemetery to the café. The cemetery was in the middle of the city. And, on that day, the café was crowded.

———

He heard a dog bark. He heard the walls of his apartment crack, or settle. He would often sit in his apartment and stay up till very late at night.

———

She was on the sidewalk, actually. And maybe she had, in fact, arrived on time. Or maybe she was, simply, this time, arriving late for their meeting. And, at that point, it was difficult to tell. He was sure, certain, however, that he could see her from where he was standing.

A large explosion rocked the city.

He sat in the café, or restaurant, and waited. He was supposed to be meeting her at the café, or restaurant. There was supposed to have been a meeting at the café, or restaurant, but he was late, or she was late. Somehow, someone was, uncharacteristically, late.

It is after the funeral, and his friends, associates, approach the café from the sidewalk. They enter through the front door. And, on that day, the café is crowded.

At home in his apartment at night, he was often tired. And there was something, a foreign object, some foreign matter, something, in his eye. He took out a handkerchief and tried to remove whatever it was that was in his eye.

And the funeral was a solemn event, an occasion, a funeral.

His friends, associates, leave the cemetery. They walk down the street, and enter a café. It is a short distance, a pleasant walk, on most days, from the cemetery to the café.

And there were others, strangers, if you will, other attendees at the funeral, strangers, observers, recorders, if you will. And there were flowers. Real flowers, and artificial ones, too. Arrangements of flowers, floral arrangements, really, or bouquets, set along the grass.

After several minutes he started to cry. It was different, then, suddenly different, things were different and he didn't know why. He felt despair, real despair, and that, in and of itself, was something new, was enough to make him cry.

He thought of her often, then, in those days, thought of her as often as he thought of anything else. He thought about her all the time. And he'd had a job, too, doing something, something important, something that needed doing, something that needed to be done.

And if it were possible to dream, to imagine, and not be scared or frightened. And if it were possible to know, at least once in a while, to picture beforehand, what the future held in store.

Still, he was sad. Really sad. And this was an unusual condition for him. He had not, in fact, been one for sadness, or for tears, not for sadness, in the least.

There was a time when he'd been happy, and even after. But there was music, and there was someone singing, or the sound of singing, somewhere, or in the train station, in the dream he'd had.

―

And his friends, associates, hold their glasses up. Or they hold their water glasses, and coffee mugs, and tea cups up high. They make a toast with a variety of beverages in their hands. And there had been a plan, an arrangement, to meet at the café. And the plan, the arrangement, to meet at the café after the funeral, had, in fact, been made before the funeral had taken place.

3

There were icons in the backyard. Not really icons, but things, objects, a collection of some sort, things, icons, really. And the sight of it, that collection of objects, those things, objects, icons, really, reminded him of death. It was late one night, really, it was night and he was tired, but he didn't go to sleep. The idea of food bothered him, attracted him, and bothered him. He'd eaten in a restaurant, had, earlier that night, eaten alone in a restaurant. And the things, the collection of objects, the icons, the plants and trees and flowers, in the backyard, and on the streets, everywhere, all of it, those things, reminded him of death.

———

There was a dog on the street. The dog was running down the street. The dog did not appear to be in distress in any way, yet, still, there was something about the sight of the dog that bothered him.

———

It was a large event, an occasion, a funeral. And there were many friends, associates, and relatives, and others, other people, who stood in the open air that day. There was the sound of the eulogy and the sound of the prayers. The sound of crying. A body was being buried, interned. It was a solemn occasion, a funeral, an event, that had required planning.

———

There had been the threat of death for years, even the threat of death, specifically, on certain occasions. And there was something in his eye, something small, an object, something foreign, some foreign matter in his eye that, from time to time, bothered him.

———

The sad part was that it was not a significant event. The funeral, in fact, was not a significant event at all.

———

And still there was a question of waiting. There was waiting to be done, always plenty of waiting to be done. He'd waited for her by the door of the café. On another occasion he'd waited for her on the street. On still another occasion he'd sat and waited for her at a table in the restaurant. And, then, in those days, he was usually on time, or, often, early, when he'd had an arrangement to meet with someone.

———

The icons, the things, the collection of objects, the things, icons, really, in the backyard reminded him of death. It had been months, or years, it had been long, had been a long time, since he'd been in that neighborhood, in that part of the city, in the backyard, at night. And there was more, there was, of course, much more to say about the situation, about all the situations he found himself in, but there was something in the way. A truck or car, or bus, something, a vehicle of some sort, was blocking his way. He was standing in the middle of the street, waving, gesturing, wildly, somewhat wildly, humiliatingly, in a way, doing a kind of dance, almost a dance, trying to catch their attention, but there was something in the way.

———

They, his friends, associates, enter the café through the front door. The door that faces the street.

―

The day he'd waited for her had turned out badly. It was bad, a bad day. Yet it was a day, a period of time, that he knew, somehow, just knew, understood, to be significant. In fact, he'd been aware that it, the day, the days, those days, in general, meant something, still he couldn't see any way of going back, of returning, to where he'd been before. Things seemed to get worse after that, though he'd expected, had, of course, expected things to get better.

―

He was waiting for her in the café, or restaurant. It was late one night, and he was tired. And, at that point, anyone would have been tired. Still, there was no way of avoiding it. This fact. The signs. There was an open door, a green, or red, door. He walked through the open door and into a great room. The room was filled with light. It was filled with the most beautiful light he had ever seen. And there had to be something to fill the days. There had to be some miracle in the works, something. Something good was about to happen. He just knew it. Or, the way he looked as he stood, standing.

―

And there are strict rules, laws, directives, strict prohibitions, governing the handling of human remains. There were complications, however. Things happened unexpectedly. And the complications appeared, or things changed, literally, overnight.

―

He could see his friends, associates, turn the corner and approach the front door of the café. He waved, gestured, wildly, somewhat wildly, humiliatingly, in a way, did a kind of dance, almost a dance, trying to get their attention.

———

There were icons, things, objects, a collection of some sort, things, icons, really, all around the backyard. It was night, and dark, and there was very little wind. He was visiting a neighborhood, a part of the city. It was dark, very dark, much darker than he was accustomed to. He was standing in the backyard and there were various objects, icons, things, a collection of some sort, things, icons, really, hanging from beams, and from walls, and on the ground: wind chimes and small statues, a stone turtle, and other things, objects, icons, really.

———

His friends, associates, sat at a table in the café. And the café was very beautiful, at that point. Still, there was something wrong, or there was something missing. There was the feeling, generally, generally speaking, that there was something wrong, that something was, in fact, missing, or even stolen, perhaps.

———

He sat and looked out the café window. He sat for a long time and stared out the front window of the café, the one that faced the sidewalk and the street.

———

And it was not long after that. The funeral.

———

It was early, or late, and it was time for him to go. He had to leave his place. He left his place early, or late, or it could have been at night, or in the evening. He went to work. He was on his way to do his job. And, on that day, things were indeed bound to change. Yet, still, at that point, there was time. There was still time. He had time, then, at that point. Time to spare. He bought stamps, and stamped a letter, and put the letter in a mailbox. And then he'd gone to work, had gone to do his job. It was later that day. It was after work. And there were stamps in his wallet. He'd intended to take the stamps out of his wallet and put them away in a drawer. Yet each time he'd opened the drawer, opened his wallet. And that day had been a surprise. It was so unpredictable. The ways the day, any day, could possibly go. There was a collision, of sorts, a violent collision, on the street outside the café. And earlier that day, he'd waited for her on the street.

———

He sat in the café, or restaurant, and waited.

———

And there were others at the funeral, others, observers, recorders, if you will. And then there was the sound of glass breaking. The sound, somewhere, off in the distance, perhaps, of glass breaking.

———

The icons, the things, the collection of objects, the things, icons, really, in the backyard were made of wood and metal, mostly, or mostly made of wood and stone, or mostly made of plastic, or made of plastic and wood and metal and stone, and even ceramic and some glass. And there was no denying that something significant had happened, that, indeed, something had changed. He bought stamps in the morning on his way to work.

———

In the meantime, there were arrangements, preparations, to be made. It was a solemn occasion, a funeral, an event that had required planning.

———

There was a dog on the street. There was a dog running down the street, and the dog was not in distress, or did not appear to be in distress, in any way. The dog ran up the street, seemingly carefree, in, seemingly, a carefree manner, yet, still, there was something sad in the way the dog ran. To him, there was a sadness, a real and profound sadness, in the way the dog ran up street. Yet, he was not, typically, one to feel sentimental over animals. He had no particular appreciation for animals, had never really paid that much attention to animals. There was a room, and he tried to see what the room looked like. There was a bed in the room, and a chair, and bookcases. Most likely, the room he slept in. The room where he spent his time. He feels that the most likely answer is that he had happened upon the room where he slept. The room where he spent his time. It was difficult to see in the dark, however. But after staring at the room for a while, he was sure that it was the place. Still, at one time, he feels, the room might have been slightly different, maybe painted a different color. Or there might have been different furniture.

4

When he sits. When he'd sat at the table. When he sits at the table, he does not quite get to say what he's been planning to say, what's been on his mind. He forgets. He's forgotten what he was going to say, what's been on his mind. When he sits at the table, he even forgets the little things. His dislikes, for instance. The way he dislikes certain things, like certain mannerisms, or gestures, the little ways in which things are expressed. And, thus, the moment is golden. And there is red in the room, and everywhere else, it seems. Indeed, he is in his element, perfectly composed, and there is no other reason to be there, or to be anywhere other than where he is at that moment. Then someone whispers from behind him, whispers, or whistles, from the back of the room. And, at that moment, in retrospect, at that golden moment, he feels that he is supposed to be there. He feels that the room, where he is, at that moment, is the place he is supposed to be. And, this time, nothing has stopped him from being in the room. And, this time, there are signs everywhere, he feels, telling him that he is, in fact, in the right place.

He is sitting at a table in the café, or restaurant. He is alone at a table in a café, or restaurant, and he is drinking coffee. He sits and drinks coffee alone at a table in the café, or restaurant.

And there is to be a meeting among his friends, associates. His friends, associates, are going to be meeting for lunch at the café.

Going deeply into things. He feels. Doing well. Not fighting. And it merely seems to be the way that things tend to go, from time to time, that bothers him. In fact, there are certain things, occurrences, trends, or tendencies, if you will, that bother him, from time to time, but only when he thinks about them. He has reached the halfway point in his cup of coffee. He is drinking coffee, now, at this time, and this particular cup has reached the proper, or, perhaps, best, temperature for drinking. There is a cup in his hands. He is holding his cup of coffee and thinking, but also watching the door. He is waiting for her at the café, or restaurant.

His friends, associates, sit at a table in the café. They sit at the table and drink coffee, tea, and various other beverages, a variety of beverages, if you will. And, at some point, someone lifts a glass and suggests that a toast be made.

And there is no smoke in the café, at that point. And no smoke outside either. And the day is neither hot nor cold.

He is drinking coffee in a café, or restaurant. And he is responsible, he feels. Still, nevertheless, he is, more or less, surprised. He is, in fact, more or less, surprised because events have taken him by surprise. And, indeed, things have changed.

He is drinking coffee in a café, or restaurant.

It is after the funeral, and his friends, associates, have gathered at the café for a meeting.

———

There is a long expanse of grass in the cemetery. The cemetery grass is, generally, well kept, cut and watered often. Each day large and small groups of people, mourners, and others, converge around the various plots set into the cemetery grass. There are often cars parked on the road that runs alongside the large expanse of grass. The cemetery is located in the middle of the city.

———

And as he sits and waits for her in the café, or restaurant, he thinks of certain things, remembers certain things. And there is much for him to remember, to keep track of, at that point.

———

There are trees in the part of the city that immediately surrounds the cemetery. There are trees and narrow, but picturesque, streets. The part of the city that immediately surrounds the cemetery is characterized by its trees and the distinctive red brick walls that line the narrow, but picturesque, streets. Indeed, the whole area, that part of the city, due primarily to the large number of distinctive red brick walls that line the narrow, but picturesque, streets, has a, more or less, quaintly industrial feel about it.

———

He is wearing a hat as he walks down the street. He has no hat. He is on his way to the café to meet his friends, associates, for lunch. He is walking down the street in a part of the city that has a, more or less, quaintly industrial feel about it. He is in the city, and he is going to meet her at the café, or restaurant. And it is still, in fact, hard to believe, sometimes. It is indeed still, sometimes, hard to believe that what has happened has, in fact, happened. It is a surprise, in the way that many events in the past months, and weeks, and days, have been a surprise. It is a surprise, he feels, and a shame, somewhat. It is a shame, somewhat, because there are things that could have been done differently. There are things, he feels, that could have been done that would have made all the difference in the world. But then, of course, nothing could have been done. Still, he stands very well. He cuts a fine figure as he walks down the street. It is his defining moment. A golden moment, if you will. Yet things could have been very different, he feels.

He is standing in the middle of the street. He is standing on an island, a concrete pedestrian traffic island, in the middle of the street. He is waving to his friends, associates, gesturing, somewhat wildly, humiliatingly, in a way, doing a kind of dance, almost a dance, trying to get their attention.

His friends, associates, are talking and drinking a of beverages in the café. It is after the funeral, and the café is, more or less, crowded that day.

And, at that point, the café, or restaurant, is, more or less, crowded. Yet, there is no music and, certainly, no dancing taking place at that time.

It is crowded in the café that day, especially, it seems, in the hours after the funeral. His friends, associates, arrive at the café. It is a beautiful day and many people are seated at tables and many more people stand at the bar.

There is something, an object, or something, in the rear of the room, in back, behind, or near, his table at the café, or restaurant. A package, perhaps, or a red bag. The red bag, or, perhaps, package, has, apparently, been left, or forgotten, by its owner. The bag, or package, is a deep and, somewhat, loud red. The bag is, in fact, striking for how loud it is, its extremely bright red color. The bag is ugly. The bag, the red bag, or package, is neither conspicuously new nor conspicuously old. The bag is a loud, or bright, red and is made of a type of leather-like material that appears to have a fair amount of wrinkles.

———

He is seated at a table at the café, or restaurant, thinking about the future. The ways in which his life has changed abruptly, unexpectedly. He is sitting at a table in the café, or restaurant, and he is surprised, and saddened, a little, by the way things have changed. Indeed, what has occurred, generally, is, more or less, a surprise. It is truly surprising, or events have, somehow, in the end, taken him by surprise.

———

And as his friends, associates, sit at a table at the café and talk and drink a variety of beverages, someone raises a glass and suggests that a toast be made. It is after the funeral and his friends, associates, are sitting at a table at the café. It is afternoon. The café is very crowded. There has been a funeral that morning.

———

It is not raining outside. In fact, the weather has been perfectly fine, seasonable. Unseasonably cool, perhaps, but nice, nonetheless.

———

He is standing in the middle of the street, and he is running late. It is unusual for him to be late. In fact, he is normally on time, or even early, when he has a plan, an arrangement, to meet with someone. And, on that day, he is supposed to be meeting someone at the café, or restaurant.

He sees her approach the café, or restaurant. It is a cold and windy day, and he is wearing a scarf and a long winter coat. Someone nearby is holding a red bag. He has dropped his bags, his packages, what appears to be his winter shopping in the middle of the street. It is a cold and windy day, and, indeed, because of the cold and wind, especially the wind, he feels, she is not able to hear him when he calls her name. He is waving at someone, gesturing, somewhat wildly, humiliatingly, in a way, doing a kind of dance, almost a dance, in the middle of the street. And, at this point, it is not clear whether she is just entering or just leaving the café, or restaurant. He can, in fact, see her from where he is standing in the middle of the street. There is someone nearby holding a red bag. He is waiting for the light to change, for the traffic to stop, so he can cross the street. But something is wrong. There is no question that something is wrong, he feels.

He is walking and reaches for his glasses in his coat pocket. He is walking on a tree-lined and narrow, but picturesque, street. Red brick walls run along one side of the street. Indeed, that part of the city is characterized by its trees and the distinctive red brick walls that line the narrow, but picturesque, streets. In fact, the whole area, that part of the city, due primarily to the large number of distinctive red brick walls that line the narrow, but picturesque, streets, has a, more or less, quaintly industrial feel about it.

5

He was standing in the backyard, thinking about laundry, not really thinking about laundry, but, still, standing in the backyard with this thought, this consideration, laundry, or not really laundry, somehow present in his mind. It was evening, really it was late at night. It was getting to be late at night.

———

And there were icons in the backyard, things, objects, a collection of some sort, things, objects, icons really, all around the backyard. It was night, getting to be late at night, and there were bugs, or insects, many, many bugs, or insects, on the ground, and there was something, in fact, wild, lush, in its way, about the whole scene, something wild, lush, about it, the scene, in its way, even though there was no wind, and even though it was getting to be late at night.

———

Then, one day, it occurred to him. The realization came quickly. He would have to do something. He would have to make a decision. He felt full, sated, as he left the café, or restaurant. He walked down the street alone. He was happy, and filled with despair, happy and sad and hopeless at the same time. There were cars on the street, but the sidewalk was empty. It was difficult and strange, and a bit complicated, his being alone, at that point. He thought about the neighborhood, that neighborhood, that part of the city, the backyard, its wildness, how lush it was, in its way.

———

As he stood in the backyard thinking, but not really thinking, about laundry, he hoped that he would, at some point, get the opportunity to reflect, to consider, to simply remember, perhaps, where it was he stood. The night was starless and beautiful. There was no one else around. The neighborhood, that neighborhood, that part of the city, the backyard, was always very quiet at night. He remembered that much. He would always, it seemed, remember that much. The way the neighborhood, that part of the city, was always very quiet at night. And how it would sometimes get very cold. He would stand in the backyard for hours, stand in the cold for hours, and look at the stars. And one could see stars then. One could see stars quite clearly from where he was standing. Yet, still, things had changed. It had been years since he'd stood in the backyard at night. And things had indeed changed, changed a great deal, but the backyard, the neighborhood, that neighborhood, that part of the city, was still the same, was still very much the same.

There is a car on the street. A car, specifically, or a truck, perhaps, or some other kind of vehicle. A specific car, or, perhaps, truck is blocking his way. A red bag. A red, or green, door.

He is standing in the middle of the street. He is standing on the concrete pedestrian island in the middle of the street. It is already past noon, and he is supposed to be meeting his friends, associates, for lunch at the café, but he is running late.

The days are passing quickly. He still has much to do, however, and, at that point, he must get to the café on time. There is to be an important meeting, and he must get to the café on time.

———

He is waiting to meet her at the café, or restaurant.

———

It is an important meeting. And it is, in fact, critical that he make it to the meeting on time. And he is normally on time, or even early, especially when he has a plan, an arrangement, to meet with someone.

———

There is a unique quality to the sky, the light of the sky, that night. In fact, there is something unique about the quality of the sky, the light of the sky, that night. And there is something special, a somewhat different, or, perhaps, unique, quality about the sky, the light of the sky, that night. Indeed, there is something different about the sky that night. And this is simply because the day has changed. For better or worse, the day has changed and, because of this, there is something different about the sky, or the light of the sky, something different about the world in general at that point. There is, in fact, something new, or some new quality, somehow, present in the world, and this difference, this change, is something that he is, inevitably, unable to appreciate, or apprehend, fully. Or, rather, his part. Indeed, it is as if something that was once clear has now stopped being clear. And then he puts his hands out, and stares at his fingers. He is standing in the backyard and staring closely at his fingers. He has seen his fingers, his face and his body, before, of course. He has, of course, appreciated, fully apprehended, the way his body looks many, many times before. How he moves his fingers, his hands, sometimes, when he speaks, and, sometimes, when he orders his meals. He has noticed, apprehended fully, all of these things. And he is not afraid. There is, in fact, no reason for him to be afraid, he feels. No reason to be afraid at that particular time.

———

101

And it had been years since he'd stood in the backyard, in that neighborhood, in that part of the city, at night.

And indeed there is something special, some special quality, perhaps, in the air that night. But he is grateful for how cool it is, for how cool the air feels on that particular night. The days pass. And there is a feeling of happiness, even contentment, in him, sometimes. He feels it. Yet at other times he is full of despair, sadness and or despair. He is sitting in a café, or restaurant, and trying to decide, trying to consider. He is trying to decide what he will eat, what he is hungry for. And he thinks, then, for a moment, that it has been a mistake to come and eat at a café, or restaurant, at all. He begins to think. He looks out the window. At the window, specifically. How the window is held in place by a painted wooden frame. He is looking at the frame, its green, or red, color, looking at the window, the way it's held in place.

And the conversation begins slowly, awkwardly, even though there is a lot to say, and even though there is very little time left to say it in.

There is the smell of smoke. Somewhere. And fire. There is the smell of smoke and fire in the air.

It is after the funeral. The friends, associates, and relatives, and others, the other people who have attended the funeral, walk across the large expanse of grass. Some walk to cars while others follow the road that leads to the main gate, the cemetery exit.

And if there is nothing left, no sign of life, he will go, exit, but he has to figure out how this is done, he feels. He has to figure out the way. The way he would go. The ways a person could possibly go. The day has been spent, squandered, wasted really, he feels, and it really is a kind of spending, his wasting the day. He feels. The days. And he has found himself in this place, in a, somewhat, familiar place. It is, in fact, a very small backyard, decorated, typically, with icons, things, or objects, a collection of some sort, things, or objects, icons, really, and it is a surprise and a shock to find himself standing alone in the backyard, in the neighborhood, in that neighborhood, in that part of the city, at night.

And a little later on, a little later in the day, or in the evening, he is able to order his coffee. He is, in fact, able to go out, or, in a sense, go on. And there is a bit of someone else's food on the table, and he takes his handkerchief out of his back pocket and wipes the food away. Still, he has a confession to make. At that point, he feels there is something he would like to confess. He would like to tell someone how he feels, but then he thinks of something else, his coffee, or, rather, the temperature of his coffee, how this particular cup of coffee has reached the proper, or, perhaps, best, temperature for drinking at that moment.

It is late afternoon and his friends, associates, have parted, have gone their separate ways. They have left the café and have, perhaps, returned to their homes, or have, perhaps, continued on to other places, other destinations.

And it is, sometimes, hopeless to try and convince, persuade, people of anything, he feels. Sometimes, he feels, it just cannot be done.

The café, or restaurant, door creaks, or squeaks, rather loudly, whenever it is opened or closed.

And there is a sound, a motorized, or, rather, mechanical, sound, in fact, the sound of work, or labor, in its way, as the casket is lowered into the ground by pulleys.

The friends, associates, and relatives, and others, the other people who have attended the funeral, walk across the cemetery grass. They do not say much to one another, at first, although a few have, in fact, whispered to one another almost continuously throughout the funeral.

At first it is hot, and then it is cold.

And there is smoke in the air, somewhere, and fire.

Still, there is something different about that night, something different, unique, in a way, about that night and about the nights that have immediately preceded it. He continues his walk because he has not yet reached his destination. Thus, he has decided to proceed. And in fact, it is too late to leave, stop, but he must get out, go out, get away, for at least a little while, he feels.

There is smoke in the air, somewhere, and fire. He can, in fact, smell the smoke as he walks down the street and past the front door of the café.

He'd waited to talk to her. He'd waited until he could not wait any longer. There was nothing he could do. He had to leave his place, get up, go outside. Still, there was no particular place to go. And now, the room is too warm. He has to go outside. He finds that he has no choice, and yet, still, he has to decide exactly where it is he's going to go.

And there is a special quality. Something, perhaps, unique. The funeral is, in its way, impressive. The funeral is, in fact, what it is. What it is supposed to be. A solemn occasion, an event, a funeral.

He is in the city and speaking to her. He is speaking to someone, to one of his friends, associates, to his friend, or associate. And he and his friend, associate, are not in the café, but are, instead, in a more or less expensive restaurant. He asks her a question—what she will have to eat. And she answers. And he is thinking of the cat he used to have. His old cat. And he is considering other matters as well as they sit across from one another at a table in a more or less expensive restaurant. Still, there is something, some determination, some shape given to. What could possibly be. And, indeed, it is difficult. And the question is difficult to answer, made especially difficult to answer because he has chosen to come to this place. And he has, in a sense, decided, or made a decision, at that point.

6

There is death to consider. It comes, sometimes, this consideration, comes, sometimes, out of the blue. In houses, in cars, on the street, while he is standing in the backyard. He had a picture, or there was a picture, or there had to be something, some way in, but the way in was unknown. It reminded him of a story he'd heard. And the end was near, and he had no business being there, and he had no business being anywhere else. And, then, just like that, it exploded. A large explosion rocked the city. A mysterious explosion. And there really was no reason to wait as long as he did. His coffee was cold. The other patrons in the café were not that friendly. Somehow, and he wasn't sure how. Or he'd dropped something, had, perhaps, uncharacteristically, left his glasses behind, had misplaced them, had, maybe, forgotten them at the table. And there were other things to consider as well. A page turning, or turning over a new leaf. The café's windows, the glass of the windows, the view, the scene through the windows. All of the wonders of the world, and he had to tell her, he was compelled to let her know what was on his mind.

And if it had rained. If there had been rain in the cemetery that day, things might have been different.

A crowd of people are standing. They are nicely dressed. And there is no rain, no rain, there is no rain.

And if his friends were good, if they were good friends. And his friends, associates, made a plan, an arrangement. And the plan was made even before the funeral, the plan, arrangement, to go and meet in the café after the funeral.

All of his friends, his good and best and lifelong friends, associates, friendships, associations, that had actually lasted until the end of his life. It was a kind of condition, this remembering, this missing the boat, this continuing, this going on, but still missing the boat, still missing the point. And if only there had been rain, even a drop of rain, a slight drizzle, anything, it might have helped. Still, it was, of course, apparent in the way he walked. His finest hour. A conclusion, or a golden moment, of sorts.

He was waiting for her in the café, or restaurant. And that day, it was not raining, there were no clouds in the sky, not a hint of rain, not a thought of rain. And he wouldn't have minded one bit if it had been raining.

Over the clouds he can see a picture. Or, to be precise, he can see a picture through the clouds, or, rather, in the clouds. He can see a picture somewhere. He has, he'd had, the ability to see these kinds of things, pictures, in places, on things, like clouds. Pictures in the clouds. But this was not a moment for reflection. There was nothing he was reflecting on at that moment. Only a particular desire, or a specific wish, for something different, a little different, a change, perhaps, or a hint that things were, in fact, moving towards the fulfillment of what he might have wished for. But the thought of his dreams. His daydreams coming true. The coming true of his dreams, this thought, however vague and ill-defined, he feels, could have been the key, the very thing that served him, served him well.

This time. He was alone. He waited alone in the middle of the street. And there was no one else around. He wasn't sure whether he was early or late, whether he was on time or not on time. He stood in the middle of the street and waited for the traffic to clear, waited until it was safe for him to cross the street.

The cars leave the cemetery slowly, and though most of the drivers are indeed in a hurry to get away, to exit the cemetery, there is no speeding, no passing, and certainly no honking of horns.

His friends, associates, and relatives, and other people, the people who have attended the funeral, walk slowly, leave the cemetery slowly, mostly with their eyes cast down. Theirs is a solemn walk, a walk taken in perfect solemnity. And it is a wonder, this walking of theirs, it is a wonder that there has been no training. No one has trained them to walk this way, with this perfect solemnity, and at such a slow and deliberate pace.

Still, it is strange, he feels, sometimes, the way things work. He often notices this about himself, this feature, or trait. He will notice something, some strange occurrence, or some coincidence, or some set of circumstances that seem to somehow connect, that is, he will notice, observe, sometimes. Observe. This.

———

It is crowded in the café. Even from across the street it is easy to see that the café is crowded. There are many people sitting at tables and many more people standing at the bar.

———

He hopes he is not late. And it is unusual for him to be late. In fact, he is usually on time, or, often, early, when he has an arrangement to meet with someone.

———

The night is dark. It is a starless night, and there are many things on his mind. He is not sure of how he has reached this point, of how he has come to stand where he does. He is not sure. He has returned. He is in the backyard, and many things have changed, no one can deny that many things have changed, but, still, the neighborhood, that part of the city, the backyard, is just the same.

———

The backyard, the neighborhood, that part of the city, is, in fact, lush with flowers and plants and trees. Indeed it is almost a jungle compared to where he lives now. In the city. Where he once lived.

———

And there is no one else around. There are no people around, in that place, at that particular time.

———

Still, he is not exactly sure of what is meant by the concept of failure. That is, he is not yet convinced that he has failed. He has failed before. He is, of course, willing to admit that. He has, in

109

fact, failed many, many times before, but still the concept of failure does not make sense, not at that point, and this only because he may or may not have succeeded. Yet, there is an idea, or image, an idea, or image, of failure that, from time to time, may or may not come to his mind. It is a shame, somewhat. And the thought, the very idea, of failure seems to be one that most people understand, one that, he feels, most people are easily able to recognize. And when he thinks this way. Thinks about failure. However, it is not the time to think such thoughts, he feels. It is, in fact, not the time for such considerations. It is a brand new day, and he has the world before him. It is glorious and new, this day, and he is marching to the beat of his own drum. Still, there is no denying that he has reacted strangely, no denying that the whole situation has had a strange effect on him, but it is not for lack of trying, and it is not because he is somehow bad, because he has done badly, rather, it is the shape of the world, the way he thinks, what he chooses to consider, what he has come up against, time and time again, that bothers him. And the rest is about facing the future. The shock of the future. And then there is the future to consider, he feels.

He leaves a note with the waiter. He is well known at the café, or restaurant, and he leaves a note with the waiter. She has not shown up for their meeting. He has waited for her, but she has not shown up.

He leaves a note with the waiter, and goes outside into the rain. It is raining, and the rain has come unexpectedly, like it does sometimes in that part of the country, in that part of the world. He turns his collar up and walks quickly. It seems like the right thing to do, walking quickly, even though he has nowhere in particular to go. He is trying to reach the train station. He is trying to get home, trying to get to work. It is past his bedtime, or he is trying to think of something in particular, trying hard to remember a particular fact, or event, or situation. He is trying hard to focus his thoughts on specific things and not allow his mind to wander. It is not early, and it is not late. He has had some time to think, at that point, to rest, stop. He has, in fact, had some time to consider where it is he plans to go. He is trying to get to the train station, but he is not sure if this is right either. If this is, in fact, the right time for that destination.

There is a police officer standing near him on the traffic island, on the concrete pedestrian island in the middle of the street. The police officer is young, and he is directing traffic. The police officer is young and inexperienced at directing traffic, and, because of this, primarily because of this, he feels, because of the police officer's inexperience at directing traffic, it is taking an unusually long time for him to cross the street.

7

And even if they were after him, even if they, his friends, associates, had come looking for him, he would not have known what to do. It would have seemed like a breach, a break, in the spirit of things, in the pattern of life, that had existed up to that point. And when he looks up, he sees his face reflected in the glass of the café, or restaurant, window.

And, this time, there are flowers in the café as well, flowers on and around the table, with some of the flowers, perhaps a bouquet, or an arrangement or two, placed nearer to the bar.

And it is hard to keep walking. It is getting harder to find a place to rest, stop. It is getting harder and harder to concentrate. He is walking. There are pedestrians on the sidewalk and cars in the street, faces everywhere he looks. The faces could, of course, mean something to him, would, of course, normally, mean something to him, but they do not, in fact, register in any special way at that time. Indeed, nothing seems to register in any special way at that time. He is not at home. He is standing in the backyard, looking at the bugs, or insects, the many, many bugs, or insects. The bugs, or insects, in the backyard are especially active at night, motivated as they tend to be, by the yellow light, or, specifically, by the light from the yellow light bulb in the backyard. And their movement, the way the bugs, or insects, move, could easily mean something, could easily register in some special way. But it is time for him to go, or move, he feels.

———

For a long time, he was waiting. At first, he'd waited in the café, or restaurant, and then he'd waited on the street.

———

And his friends, associates, and relatives, stand together on the neatly cut cemetery grass. There are others, other people, at the funeral as well, strangers, it seems, who attend the funeral, who often attend funerals, and other events, as observers, as recorders, if you will.

———

The morning comes and another morning comes and then another morning comes and he realizes that he has not been home for a long time. Indeed, there has been an abrupt shift in the world, and, thus, in his way of looking at the world. And, indeed, it is true that things have, in fact, changed. And this new condition, what the world has become, his new perspective, is serious. The change is, in fact, serious, and his recognition of it, however long delayed, propels him into a kind of shock. But it is the jar of marmalade on the café table that attracts him more than anything else. Not really, but this is what he feels, for a moment, before he looks out the window. It is hot, and then it is cold. He is not at home. He is on the street and waiting, and then he is on the street and walking. It is a circumstance, a new circumstance, he finds himself in. He is in a circumstance that he would never have expected to occur. And after a day, after one week, or more, when more than one day, or week, has passed, the shock, or the recognition of the shock, or the recognition, finally, that something has changed, becomes even more apparent. And despite this, this delayed recognition, or prolonged failure to understand, to admit, the truth. His part. The days have continued to pass. Indeed, there has already been a lapse of time. It is a disappointment. And he is shocked when he looks at himself in the mirror, when he sees himself reflected in the glass.

———

As he turns his head, as he waits to cross the street, simply to cross the street, he sees faces, and, for a moment, he understands. Something new, something novel, has occurred.

———

There are faces framed by car windows, faces framed by the low hanging branches of trees on the street, faces framed by doorways and by windows. And, for a moment, he is excited. He gestures wildly, waves, does a kind of dance, almost a dance, from the concrete pedestrian island in the middle of the street, trying to get their attention.

———

And it is evident that the cemetery grass has been well cared for, cut often, that indeed the cemetery itself is, somehow, if you will, nice, or pleasant, in its way. The cemetery is, in fact, a pleasant and well cared for place.

———

The funeral is large. By anyone's standards it is a large funeral. Well attended.

———

And it is hard to imagine anything good. He is having a hard time imagining how anything good will come out of the new circumstance, his new perspective, the new and changed world, he finds himself in. He is suffering, and the reason for his suffering, if there is a reason, is unknown. It is an unknown, the reason for his suffering. And if he were able to rest, stop, to really rest, stop, whether on the street or somewhere else inside, perhaps, to rest, stop, long enough to consider the reason, the possible reason, or reasons, why.

―――

Indeed, the days have turned strange. And, indeed, something unexpected has occurred. And it is now, or it can now be considered, he feels, more or less, a time of crisis. Indeed, there is, as there often is, somewhere, even in many places at once, it seems, a crisis. In fact, there is a crisis at home, or, maybe, a crisis, of some sort, abroad. There is, in any case, it seems, definitely, a crisis somewhere, at that time.

―――

And, yet, there is nothing special about the morning. The morning, that morning, is the same as many other mornings, he feels. Yet that day, on that morning, the feeling is different. And, at that time, the morning is not the same, mainly because the circumstances have changed. Indeed, it is the same world, and, yet, the color of the sky, or its light, the quality of light, has, in fact, changed.

―――

He is on the street. He has just returned to work, and he is on the street. He is back where he belongs, in familiar territory, he feels. He lights a cigarette and stands by a wall at the end of the street, not far from the café. Or he, in fact, has no cigarettes and there is smoke in the air. In either case, there is a wall at the end of the street, not far from the café. The wall is made of red brick and has a quaintly industrial feel about it. Indeed the red brick wall gives the entire area surrounding the café a quaintly industrial feel. And he needs to get home as soon as possible, he feels.

It is after the funeral. His friends, associates, and relatives, and others, the other people who have attended the funeral, walk across the large expanse of grass. Some walk to cars while others follow the road that leads to the cemetery's main gate.

First it is hot, and then it is cold.

There is a crowd in the café at that moment, at that time. His friends, associates, sit at the table and eat bread and cheese. They sit at the table together and eat bread and a variety of cheeses. And then there are drinks as well. His friends, associates, sit at the table and eat and drink and talk.

And as he walks, or stands, or sits, while he is sitting at the table, and is, at last, able to see, to rest, or, in a sense, stop.

He smiles and waves at his friends, associates, from the concrete pedestrian island in the middle of the street. There is often a police officer, or, sometimes, there is not a police officer. The police officer stands on the concrete pedestrian island and, it seems, monitors the traffic. He is standing next to a police officer. He sees his party, the people he is supposed to be meeting for lunch, his friends, associates, walk into a café, and he does not want to be late. Indeed, he is rarely late. In fact, he is often on time, or even early, especially when he has a plan, an arrangement, to meet with someone. There is smoke, or someone is smoking a cigarette, or rather, there is smoke either in the café or in the air outside the café. And there is a party, or there is some other type of activity, something out of the ordinary, going on in the café at that time. There are flowers in the café. It is later. And, in the end, there is not going to be enough time for him to say what he'd been meaning to say. He realizes, begins to realize, that the time is passing quickly, is going by fast, is simply flying by, and there is still something he'd been meaning to say to her. There is still something important on his mind, that needs to be said, he feels.

———

It is an old city, or there are many people in the city at that time. It is an old neighborhood in a recently redeveloped section of the city. A part of the city with a large number of red brick walls, and many cafés and restaurants. Indeed, and in large part due to the large number of red brick walls, that entire part of the city has a, more or less, quaintly industrial feel about it.

———

He has stopped to listen, or he does not, in fact, hear anything in particular. He is standing. He is standing, leaning, really, against a red brick wall at the end of the street, not far from the door of the café. And there is very little to worry about, he feels. In fact, he feels he has no special need to worry, at least not at that point.

117

8

It never varies, mostly because of the way things change. And it is certain, at this point, that many things have, in fact, changed, and this despite the way they, things, appear to be on the surface. Still, it was wrong. The way things happened was wrong. Things started out fast, and then stopped. Continued. Changed. The places. Events. The goods and services. And, at that point, his job was essentially finished. Though it, the way things happened, might have looked different from another perspective. It was nighttime. That much is clear. There was the moon in the sky. It was the middle of summer. It was the middle of winter and there was an excitement in the air. One could feel it. There was definitely something special in the air. One could feel it. There was the smell of spring. And, on one long autumn afternoon, he was alone and relaxed. For once he was alone and relaxed and in good humor. Someone would be calling him soon. It was clear. There was news on the way, the news he was waiting for, good news, and the news would come quickly. Indeed, change, it seemed, was certainly on the way.

It was late at night, and it made no difference that it was late at night. He was certain that the news, good news, would come soon, quickly, in no time. In fact, he was certain that the change he'd been waiting for was just around the corner.

Really, it was an unusual story, an unusual tale, and a sign, it seemed, of things to come. Still, there was very little to pay attention to, really, even if one had been inclined to pay attention to those types of things, to signs and such, he feels.

And then there were sounds, ominous sounds, from outside, and a cracking, or creaking, the sound of wood cracking, or creaking, from inside the house, the building, or structure, from the place where he was at that time.

It is late at night. He has returned. And soon he will stand in the backyard and smoke a cigarette, he has no cigarette, or there will be smoke in the air. And soon he will stare at the moon, the summer moon, through the trees and observe the bugs, or insects, in the yellow light, or, rather, the light from the yellow light bulb in the backyard. Still, he is not sure, not at all certain, about what he will do next, or about how things, events, will play out. And he has to stop counting. He has to stop thinking. He has to stop everything because there is, in fact, no reason for him to continue in that manner, his job being, at that point, essentially finished. And, the way he is, that is, his new perspective. There is a cracking, or creaking, sound, the sound of wood cracking, or creaking. He is thinking. He has to return, or he has, in fact, returned, but the circumstances are new. And, at that point, there is not much left to be done, his job being, at that point, essentially finished.

And even then, there is eating and there is talking and there is music, but he is not there. And how terrible it is to think of, to imagine, his not being there, he feels. And the time moves very quickly. The time goes by quickly, especially on summer nights. The way the time goes by on a winter night when the air is cold. It is warm in the summer. The summer had been especially warm. And the time has gone by, is going by, so quickly. He thinks he will go home now, and that, at some point, he should, in fact, go home. Yet home is an idea, is, or should be, the thing, is, or should be, the very thing, he feels. Still, recently he has not thought much about home. He has not, in fact, thought about going home very often at all. And home. Home. And it, home, is, or should be, a place, is, or should be, the very place, he feels. But this type of thinking suddenly feels old, archaic, in a way, and it is getting harder and harder, it seems, to get anyone else to believe in it.

———

There is a door on the street, not far from, in fact, right next to, the café. A red, or green, door. The door appears to be locked from the outside.

———

There is a cat that walks, or runs, that moves quickly, sometimes, over the cemetery grass. And there are small buildings, or house-like structures, as well, small buildings, or house-like structures, made of, mostly, polished stone, or marble, in fact, mausoleums, here and there, on the cemetery grass.

———

The cemetery has a large expanse of grass. His friends, associates, walk across the grass, briefly, it seems, and then, for a longer time, along the cemetery road. The cemetery road slopes downward in the direction they are walking and is covered with gravel, mostly, and even glass, in places, small bits of what appears to be broken glass.

———

It is a beautiful evening.

———

The funeral is over. It is after the funeral.

———

It is a beautiful spring day, not too warm, a little windy, perhaps, but still with a feeling, slightly, a feeling, or nip, if you will, of winter in the air.

———

It is winter, and it is not raining. His friends, associates, have decided to meet at the café. It is after the funeral, and his friends, associates, walk from the cemetery to the café through the cold, chill of the day.

———

It is winter. He has had a bad feeling. He has had a premonition, in a way. And, in fact, there is something strange about this night, something strange about the air, the heat, something strange about everything around him. He is certain that she will call. He is certain that she has already called, and that he has, in fact, spoken to her and that he has, in fact, said the wrong thing. Or he is unable to hear what she has said, and he forgets, forgets that the conversation has already occurred, or has not occurred. At first he tells himself to eat, but, at this point, he can barely stand up. He has no way of getting up, of getting out of bed. It is an entirely new world, a new condition, and thus a new perspective, that he faces, recognizes, for, perhaps, the first time, and, because of this, it is evident to him, at least at that point, that he is not a superman, not a superman after all. But this is a premonition. He remembers this fact. This is a premonition, and not a memory, after all. And it does not have to be this way. But his work is hard, and the time goes by so quickly. It is, therefore, easy, he feels, to feel like a failure.

121

———

There is no denying that it is often crowded on the streets of the city. And it is often crowded in the café as well. Indeed, despite the hour, and despite the time of year, and despite the unseasonable, or inclement, weather, the café is, in fact, crowded.

———

His friends, associates, sit at a table at the café.

———

He is sitting at a table at the café, or restaurant, and he is waiting. He is waiting for her to arrive. He stirs his tea, or he drinks his coffee. He lights a cigarette, he has no cigarette, or there is smoke in the air. The café, or restaurant, is crowded, and there is a great deal of smoke in the air, at that point, especially on the street, or in and around the bar.

———

There is smoke in the backyard, and bugs, or insects, many, many bugs, or insects, and he has come to the backyard from a long way away. He has come to stand in the backyard. He has come to the backyard to contemplate the moon, to think, and to view the icons, the things, the collection of objects, icons, really, in the moonlight, or, rather, by the light of the moon.

———

But there is a funeral to attend to, a funeral that requires planning. His friends, associates, and relatives, and others, will all be there, will all attend the funeral. It is, will be, a solemn occasion, an event, a funeral.

———

On this day, the café is crowded, and there is no place to sit at any of the tables. Therefore, at this time, there is nothing to do. He walks down the street. He leans against a red brick wall. He is alone. He is sticking, mostly, to a familiar path, and it is no surprise that, in the end, he feels, more or less, comfortable, in a way.

―

At the cemetery, there is a large mausoleum, larger than the rest, that sits in a secluded spot near a fountain, or pool, or near some other type of small body of water. It is, by far, the largest, and most prominent, noticeable, building, or structure, mausoleum, in the cemetery.

―

He opens the door. There is a red, or green, door on the street, not far from, in fact, right next to, the café. It is a small red, or green, door, and he has been thinking almost exclusively about the door for days, or weeks, or months. He pulls on the red, or green, door, but, again and again, as is often the case with these things, the door is locked and, therefore, does not open.

―

He is waiting, or resting, stopped, for a moment. He is about to enter the café, or restaurant. He is supposed to be meeting someone for lunch at the café, or restaurant, and he is waiting for her to arrive.

9

It was after, and not before. A starless night, or so it seemed. But that was before, yet it was always before, in its way, and, still, there was no getting around the fact that the time, or time, in general, made no, or, rather, made very little difference at all. Indeed, it was fine to ply one's trade, and, in those days, it really was fine. There was no one around to bother you. You went about your business. But still, strangers came and went, and faces appeared out of nowhere, and there was a level of commitment, then, that was, somehow, surprising, and, perhaps, just a little bit exciting. He was on the table, or he was at the table. Really, he was sitting at a table at the café, or restaurant, and trying to do his job, trying to consider how he could possibly do his job a little better, or, at least, a little more successfully, but the uncertainty, how he hesitated, was also a surprise, a real surprise, turned out to be a surprise as well.

When he put on his hat, he had no hat, he felt wise and carefree and wonderful. He put on his hat and took a walk. And this was in the beginning, during the first few days. There were buildings, then, and people on the sidewalks, and cars and traffic in the streets. It was all very exciting. And then a change came. There was one lucky day. A golden moment. There was a real voice in his head. He couldn't stop himself from thinking. And it would have been difficult, anyhow, at that point, to imagine stopping oneself from thinking. The position he was in. He was in some kind of fix. And it wasn't at all clear to those around him, his friends, associates, exactly what his situation, or, for that matter, the world's, involved.

No one, in fact, knew. A favor. He had to ask a favor, or there was something very important that he thought he had to ask her for, and this was because he had no choice, or because he had very little choice, and if there was still hope, at that point, it would have been difficult to conceive of, or, rather, difficult to imagine. A hope difficult to imagine. And then there was the whole question of his commitment, the question of his sincerity, or, really, not a question of either one of those things. It had to be the way it was. There was no getting around it. And, as a result of this, stories were often told about him. Indeed, in those days, he was often the subject of conversation, a character in stories, so to speak, especially by people in and around the café.

———

It took two weeks. And two weeks would, in fact, be long enough, he felt, to determine the answer, to determine what the proper course of action would be. It had been a long day. The two weeks, the period of crisis, had started during the day, and it was still going on, continuing, still, even though it was, at that point, night, or rather, nighttime.

———

The crisis. And there was, seemingly, always a crisis going on somewhere.

———

A large explosion rocked the city.

———

Yet the story of the crisis was not even close to ending. And, at that point, it was very uncertain, that is, the situation itself was very uncertain. And, by his reckoning, it, the period of uncertainty, or crisis, had lasted the better part of two weeks, or after two weeks, or, rather, by the end of two weeks, he would know the answer, one way or the other, he would know the answer for sure after, at the most, two weeks. In the meantime there were problems, other problems to deal with as well. There was a tear in his shirt, or he was running out of clothes, running out of good things to wear. And if he really was moving that fast, quickly, if he really was just approaching, or arriving at, the café, or, really, just leaving, exiting, the café, or restaurant, none of it made sense, not in terms of time, the situation certainly did not make sense in terms of time.

———

Still, at that point, and at that point it was easy to assign blame, it was more or less easy to assign blame, the reality of the situation not being clear, the period of crisis having not yet ended.

———

And, in the meantime, there was something bothering him, something in his eye, something, perhaps, foreign matter of some sort, or a tiny object of some kind, something irritating and slightly painful, stuck, or, rather, lodged in his eye.

———

And there was very little that, he felt, still needed to be considered about the way things, in general, were being handled, at that point. In fact, he was very sure of himself, then, or he had been much more confident, at one time.

———

And, in any case, one day, the crisis, or the period of crisis, would, in fact, come to an end.

———

It would never really end, though, that is, the period of crisis would never really end. And there was always a crisis going on, occurring, somewhere, it seemed, at some time.

———

And there were just a few last things that he had to take care of, a few last details that he still had to consider before he could finish his work and get to the café, or restaurant, on time.

———

A broken piece of glass. Or glass. Not broken glass, not exactly broken glass. And, in fact, the glass was not broken. There was, in fact, no broken glass. There was no broken glass, at that point. He'd simply left his glasses at the café. And that was it, too, the story, or what was bothering him, at first. It just sounded right. He'd left his glasses at the café, and he'd have to go back, at some point, to pick them up, to look for them. He had no choice. And even though he thought he'd remembered them, thought that, this time, he hadn't left them behind, left his glasses at the café, so to speak, he would, in fact, have to go back to the café, retrace his steps, in a way, to find them again.

———

Still, there was a feeling among those who'd attended the funeral, his friends, associates, and relatives, and others, the other people who'd attended the funeral, that the funeral itself, as far as funerals go, had been, on the whole, a success.

———

And then, one day, it, that is, things, changed. That is, something definitely changed. And, from that point on, things were, in fact, very different.

And it was painful and difficult. And it was all rather unexpected. That is, one day, things changed. One day things definitely changed. And, moreover, it, the change, came, seemingly, out of the blue.

Still, he feels that there must have been people who knew all about it. Certainly, at the very least, people must have noticed. But the time passed very slowly. And there was little, really very little, he could do about what people thought or knew. And things were, in fact, very different from that point on. And a crisis, or, rather, a change, or, perhaps, a very profound change in his life, his perspective, or in the world in general, had come, had appeared, rather unexpectedly, that is, a change had definitely come, and it had come, seemingly, out of the blue.

The house, or building, the structure, the place he occupies at that time, creaks, or cracks, makes a creaking, or cracking, sound. The house, or building, the structure, where he is, the place he occupies, at that time, is mostly made of wood. And there are bugs, or insects, many, many bugs, or insects, in the backyard.

There are icons, things, objects, a collection of some sort, things, icons, really, all around the backyard.

It is night, or, rather, nighttime, by then, at that point.

And then another day. And, then, in a real sense, another day passes.

———

He is coughing. There is something in his mouth, in his eye, some foreign matter, or a tiny object, perhaps, stuck in his mouth, his throat, at first, and then, it seems, something else stuck, or, rather, perhaps, lodged, in his eye.

———

He is walking down the street. It is a beautiful afternoon.

———

It is noon, and his friends, associates, have met at the café for a lunchtime meeting.

———

It is noon, and he is going to the café to meet his friends, associates, for a lunch meeting. He is trying to cross the street. He is, at that point, already running a little late. And the thought of his being late, or the idea, so to speak, that he is, in fact, late, is rather surprising to him. He is almost always on time, or often early, when he has made a plan, an arrangement, to meet with someone. He is walking down the street. The walls of most of the buildings he passes are made of a reddish brick, and the entire area has a quaintly industrial feel about it. It is a beautiful day in the middle of the city. It is neither too hot nor too cold. He is standing on the sidewalk, standing in front of a red, or green, door. He is standing in front of a smallish red, or green, door that is not far from, that is, in fact, right next to the café. He pulls at the handle. The door yields, gives, slightly, but is, in fact, locked. The door opens to a short flight of steps that leads to a basement room. It is a thick wooden door, red or green, depending on the season, of course, and padlocked from the outside. He pulls on the chain, pulls on the lock, tries the handle. The door yields, gives, slightly, but is, in fact, locked. He looks to the right, looks to the left. He makes sure that no one is coming, that no one is around, and then he pulls on the chain, pulls on the lock, tries the handle. Again and again, the door is locked. It is the door to a small cellar, a basement room, that the café uses for storage, mostly, and, from time to time, for other purposes as well. And, then, just like that, a feeling comes, and comes, seemingly, from out of the blue. And the world is lost. He feels. Or, for a moment, he feels that the world is lost, and that he has no purpose. Indeed, for a moment, he feels that he has no idea of why he is where he is, nor of why he's doing what he's doing. And this, the whole situation, his position, or, rather, his knowledge of it, or, rather, how he perceives it, his perspective, at that moment, is, however, as it were, not a surprise, at least he does not, at first, feel surprised by his knowledge, by what he thinks he knows, by the way he feels, but, still, a feeling has definitely come, something very different and unexpected has definitely come, and, in a way, this new thing, or, rather, this feeling that has come, is a surprise, a real surprise, turns out to be a surprise after all.

10

It is crowded in the café, or restaurant, that day. And he has had a dream, but not a dream, not really, not a dream in the strict sense of the word. And he opens his mouth. This is because he is sure that he is supposed to enter. He has pushed the red, or green, door too hard and has fallen down, or he has fallen in love. He has fallen down a flight of steps. The door that leads to the café's basement storage room is green, or red. The basement room is used for storage, mostly. The café uses this basement room for storage, mostly, it seems. But it is dirty and drab in the basement room and there is no reason for him to be there. Still, there is something familiar, something comforting, perhaps, about this place. And it is, in fact, a place, somewhere familiar, and, because of that, in a sense, comforting, perhaps. And he is trying to structure his dream around this idea. He is making a plan, a plan for his future, planning out what he will do next. But none of this is true because, somehow, he is asleep and dreaming. Still, lately, he has been having trouble concentrating. Ever since the situation, the crisis, began he has not, it seems, been able to concentrate. And this is the first time. Although the problem has been going on for months. And it is, in its way, an ongoing problem. And even when he sees them, sees the faces, sees something unexpected in the basement storage room. And even if what he sees does not necessarily fit. But, then, this is the way he thinks. And he has to try the door again. There is a light at the bottom of the stairs. He is supposed to move toward the light. He is supposed to meet someone. He is supposed to be there at a specific time, but he is late, and it is unusual for him to be late. In fact, he is normally on time, or even early, especially when he has a plan, an arrangement, to meet with someone. But it all becomes too much, he feels. The walking, climbing, down the stairs, and then even the waiting is suddenly very difficult. He can't concentrate, and the air is bad. At first it is hot, and then it is cold. It is hot that afternoon. He has sat in the café, or restaurant, for a long time. He has been waiting for her. He has sat and read several local, and national, and international newspapers. He has sat quietly and not made a sound. Yet, he will forget something, he feels. He is, in fact, sure to forget something. He is, in fact, certain that he will leave something important behind.

11

There was, in fact, nothing behind the green, or red, door. There is a green, or red, door on the street, not far from, in fact, right next to, the café. And when he'd finally opened the door, when he'd finally climbed down the stairs and stepped inside the room, there was nothing. There was really nothing behind the green, or red, door. In the end, there was, in fact, nothing.

It is not raining and there is a funeral, several funerals, actually, underway at the cemetery at that time.

The funeral, the funeral in question, was well attended. There were many friends, associates, and relatives, and others, who'd attended the funeral that day.

And it seemed very difficult to place. The smell, or odor. There was an unexpected smell, or odor, that had, somehow, permeated the world, and everything in it, it seemed, in a way. And the matter was serious, it was, in fact, not a trifling matter at all. There was a routine. And it was amazing, or it was sickening, there was something about the quality of the smell, or odor.

It was in the room, the room where he stood, or on the street. He was finding it more and more difficult to concentrate. He was never quite certain, not sure, and, at that point, his mind often wandered. It was a beautiful day in the city. There were people out and about. And he stood, or leaned, against a wall, a red brick wall on the street. The wall was very old and made of red brick and gave the entire neighborhood, that part of the city, a quaintly industrial feel.

There is a red, or green, door on the street. The red, or green, door is not far from, is, in fact, right next to, the café. He is standing on the street, waiting. It is a beautiful day in the city. The sun is out, and shining.

And it is deafening in the basement room, the one the café uses for storage, when he finally manages to get inside. The café, or restaurant, is full of people. He has been waiting for a long time. He knows now that she will not show up, that she has, in fact, missed their meeting.

There is a feeling of relief for the friends, associates, and relatives, and others, the other people who have attended the funeral, as they exit the cemetery. It, the feeling, is, it seems, in fact, perfectly natural. Still, the walk across the long expanse of grass and down the road toward the main gate of the cemetery is, in places, more or less, pleasant.

The café is in the middle of the city, not far from the cemetery. It is a relatively short walk from the cemetery to the café. And the day, that day, is beautiful. There is no rain. And the café is crowded, at that point. In fact, the café is often crowded at that time of day. His friends, associates, sit at a table and talk.

———

In terms of the weather, it has been an interesting season. In terms of the weather, it has been an interesting year. And the time has passed quickly. The weather has, in fact, been unusual, first seasonable and then, at times, unseasonable, or inclement, so to speak. And the city itself has gone through many changes over time. Indeed, conditions in the city are better or worse at any given time, depending on whom one talks to. The season has been dry, but beautiful, uncharacteristically dry, but, nonetheless, beautiful, in its way.

———

The street that runs from the cemetery to the café slopes downward. It is a pleasant and, for the most part, undemanding walk from the cemetery to the café, still, one can feel the way the street slopes downward, however slightly. Most of the buildings in that part of the city are made of a reddish brick, and the entire area has a quaintly industrial feel about it.

———

The green, or red, door does, in fact, yield, give, slightly. The green, or red, door will, in fact, yield, give, slightly, it seems, when someone pulls the handle, and this is possible even when the door is locked with a chain and padlock.

———

Still, at times, he is standing in the backyard. And the difference in landscape from one end of the city to the other is remarkable, he feels. He is in a lush environment, and, in fact, the backyard, the neighborhood, that neighborhood, that part of the city, is almost a jungle compared to where he lives now. In the city. He is standing in the backyard, looking at the many icons, the things, or objects, a collection of some sort, things, icons, really, that hang, or sit on walls, or lie about on the ground. It is a still night. And the nights, at that point, have mostly been still. The air does not, in fact, move, or moves only slightly, and, thus, the icons, the things, or objects, the collection of some sort, the things, icons, really, stand still, or hang, or lie on the ground, without moving.

He is standing in the backyard, looking at the plants and flowers, looking at the trees, looking, in fact, generally, at the lushness of the environment. And the neighborhood, that neighborhood, that part of the city, is, in general, lush. In fact, it is almost a jungle compared to where he lives now. In the city.

It is after the funeral and his friends, associates, walk across the large expanse of grass. It is a good-sized cemetery. A wrought iron gate and a red brick wall mark the cemetery's perimeter and separate it from the surrounding neighborhood in the city.

At that point, he is continually standing and waiting. He is watching, too, from certain vantage points. He is standing and waiting and watching from key vantage points, he feels, in the city. The weather has been splendid, and each day he is able to perform the same routine. There are, in fact, certain routines he performs each day. But then, one day, it stops, or his routines end. Something has, in fact, happened that has changed everything. There is a part of the city that is new and a part of the city that is old. He is standing on the street, and then, later, he is sitting in a café, or restaurant. He checks his watch and sees that he is late, or sees that he is on time, or even early, and that she is late. Someone is, it seems, uncharacteristically late. And it is unusual for him to be late. In fact, he is usually on time, or, often, early, when he has an arrangement to meet with someone.

12

It was the summer, or it was winter. And there were other variables to consider as well. Still, to think, it hadn't always been like that. To think, it hadn't always been that way. And, thinking. It was getting tiring. He found himself alone, and thinking. Somewhat lost in his own thoughts, it seemed. And it had all come about so unexpectedly in the end. In fact, things played out in a, more or less, surprising manner. And it seemed as if there were no two ways about it. Still, he couldn't exactly remember. There was an unexpected smell, or odor, that had, somehow, permeated the world, and everything in it, it seemed. And the matter was serious, it was, in fact, not a trifling matter at all. And it was amazing, or it was sickening. There was something about the quality of the smell, or odor. It was all so childish, really. Childish. He had, in a sense, become a child, too.

———

And it was, in part, because of him that the light changed. The light changed, and it was a bother. The new light, or, rather, the light's new quality, bothered people. Bothered, and frightened them, a little, it seemed. Neighbors, strangers, people on the street, people he didn't really know.

———

It was all so unexpected, really, how in the end, things played out in a, more or less, surprising manner.

———

A road runs through the middle of the cemetery, bisects it. There is a large expanse of grass on one side of the road and a, somewhat, wild, unkempt, hillside on the other. A wrought iron fence and a red brick wall form the perimeter of the cemetery and separate it from the city outside. The wrought iron fence merges with the red brick wall in places, runs along the top of the wall, here and there.

———

They are in the café, or restaurant, talking.

———

It is after the funeral.

———

They, his friends, associates, sit at a table in the café and talk. And it is not, in fact, at all clear, at that point, what they are talking about.

———

The light of the sky changed, and it was a bother. The new light, or, rather, the new quality of the light, bothered people. Bothered, and frightened them, a little, it seemed.

———

By then, at that point, in the dream he had, he has, at last, exited the train. He has been riding the city trains a great deal lately. And, suddenly, perhaps as a result of his riding the train, a new condition, or quality of life, has emerged. And this, this new condition, or quality of life, the fact of it, its emergence, is a surprise, a real surprise. For example, he has been going to the same café, or restaurant, for many years, yet on that night it all seems different. Everything seems different. Indeed, there is no question that a great deal has changed. He has exited the train, left it behind, so to speak. And he is walking, or climbing, down a steep hill, walking along a road, or a street, in the city. It is lush in that part of the city, in that neighborhood, in the backyard. In fact, it is almost a jungle compared to where he lives now. In the city. There are trees and plants and flowers, houses and buildings and other structures. The city itself has ended, or the city proper has ended, or this is, in fact, an entirely different part of the city, a different part of the same city. He is walking, or climbing, down a steep hill. And his walk, or climb, has been, it seems, well-established, has become a part of his routine. There is a neighborhood in the city filled with trees and plants and flowers, and also houses and buildings and other structures. And another neighborhood, it seems, has been cleverly built into the side of a hill. And he is marching, or there is strange music in the air, or there is no music, but merely the sounds of bugs, or insects, many, many bugs, or insects, attracted, as they tend to be, to the yellow light of the light bulb that shines in the backyard at night. He is standing in the backyard. The neighborhood, that neighborhood, that part of the city, in general, is lush. It is almost a jungle compared to where he lives now. In the city. There are trees, and bushes and flowers, a variety of plants, and places to be alone. The weather is fine. The evenings are, more or less, pleasant, and cool. And he is walking, or climbing, and thinking various things, various thoughts. The future is bright, and he will be setting himself up in such and such a way. Tomorrow is a brand new day, and there are such and such possibilities. There is a yellow light, or a yellow light bulb, in the backyard. And the bugs, or insects, the many, many bugs, or insects, move toward him when he is standing near, or, in fact, next to, the yellow light.

There are icons, things, objects, a collection of some sort, things, objects, icons, really, in the backyard. And he has walked a long way. He has walked, or climbed, down a steep hill. It is lush in the neighborhood, in that part of the city, in the backyard, at night.

It is a long walk, or climb, from the train station to the backyard. The train station itself sits at the top, or near the top, of a hill, or a small mountain, really. And he has descended, or walked, or climbed, or hiked, in a way, down a steep hill, or a small mountain, really, many many times before.

They are sitting at a table, at a, more or less, expensive restaurant. A waiter is standing next to the table and taking their orders. Earlier, the waiter had opened menus and handed the opened menus to them. And this occurs in a, more or less, expensive restaurant. And one of them does not get up from the table. One of them, it seems, stays, remains, seated. There is no one placing an order at the bar. There is a waiter holding menus. But the feeling, the mood, the tenor of the evening, has, in fact, at that point, changed.

Walking, or climbing, down the hill, sometimes one way and sometimes another way. He is deliriously happy and content, and then angry. He feels guilty, sometimes. As if his deepest and most personal secrets have all been found out. He is dreaming that he gets what he deserves. He is happy, again and again, for no apparent reason. And, moreover, a lot has been left unfinished, unsaid, he feels.

There is someone coughing in the café, or restaurant. On that day, it is crowded in the café, or restaurant. It is morning, or it is late afternoon. And it has been a long time since he has stood in the backyard. He has waited a long time for her, but she has not shown up for their meeting.

141

There is a single row of chairs and a small stand, or dais, or podium, on the grass by the gravesite. There is green grass and headstones, and friends, associates, and relatives, and others, other people, at the funeral.

His friends, associates, sit at a table in the café. It is after the funeral.

He is dreaming, but still finding it harder and harder to concentrate each time he walks, or climbs, down the steep hill. He is, however, sure of himself, at this time. There is, in fact, no doubt in his mind. And when he walks, or climbs, he is, in a sense, happy, he feels. And, in fact, this walking, or climbing, the dream of it, is, then, at that point, something good. Merely moving between one place and another is, in a sense, good. Yet, he feels that for too long a time there was nothing comparably good in his life, that is, nothing as good as walking, or climbing. He is, in fact, moving between one place and another, walking, or climbing, and it is getting harder and harder to concentrate. And, it seems, there is something in his eye, a foreign object, a speck of dust, perhaps, or dirt, some foreign matter, stuck in his eye.

There is a police officer, a traffic control officer, standing beside him in the middle of the street, on the concrete pedestrian traffic island in the middle of the street. The police officer is young and, perhaps, inexperienced.

He is standing in the middle of the street, on a concrete pedestrian traffic island in the middle of the street. He is gesturing, waving to someone, a group of friends, associates, perhaps, or he is waving to someone else, trying to catch that person's attention. He is waving, gesturing, somewhat wildly, humiliatingly, in a way, doing a kind of dance, almost a dance, trying to get their attention.

———

He is trying to balance, keep a hold of, his bags and boxes of holiday shopping as he crosses the street, or he has a bag, or there is a red bag, or he has a basket of fruit, or, rather, a large gift basket, in his hands. He is sitting at the table at the café, or restaurant, and waiting. There is a basket of fruit, or, rather, a large gift basket, on the table, or there is a red bag on the floor at the back of the café. The tables at the café, or restaurant, are filled with people. However, there is no one he knows in the café, or restaurant, at that time. He is, for all intents and purposes, alone. He gets up from the table, leaves the café, or restaurant, through the front door and goes outside. He is, it seems, restless and cannot stay inside any longer. There are too many people in the café, and there has been no music and no dancing, and he realizes that he has lost something, or he realizes that he is late. He has arrived too late for an important meeting.

———

There had been warning signs, of course. There had been warning signs for days, or weeks, or months, or years. But these signs, or warnings, had gone mostly unheeded. No one paid attention. And he has to turn around and walk, or climb, back up the steep hill and leave. He is restless and must leave that place immediately, or, rather, in a hurry.

———

He can see his friends, associates, enter the café from where he is standing in the middle of the street, the concrete pedestrian island in the middle of the street. His friends, associates, are either entering or exiting the café. Yet, at that point, it is not clear whether his friends, associates, are, in fact, entering or exiting the café.

———

It is not at all certain that he has, in fact, done anything, one way or the other. And, as a result, he feels that he has, perhaps, failed at his tasks. It has been several hours since he's left the train station.

———

Still, the day started out, in a manner of speaking, one way, and then ended up another way. Still, the day, the day in question, that day, started out, in a manner of speaking, one way, and then ended up another way.

———

He is sitting at a table in the café, or restaurant.

———

It has been a long day and he is tired, mentally, or emotionally, a bit tired, perhaps. Still, there is very little to worry about, he feels. And when he walks, or climbs, it is liberating, in a way. A waiter is handing them menus. They are in a, more or less, expensive restaurant, and, as is the custom in, more or less, expensive restaurants, the waiter opens their menus for them.

13

The neighborhood, that neighborhood, that part of the city, the backyard, was lush, almost a jungle compared to where he lived now. In the city. He often walked through the neighborhood, that neighborhood, that part of the city, at night. He often stood in the backyard. And, in fact, the neighborhood, that neighborhood, that part of the city, the backyard itself, hadn't changed all that much. Yet, each time he stood in the backyard it was, in a sense, like something new, or, in fact, a fresh start. He took the train each night in his dream. He rode the train to the station. He was, usually, often, the only passenger on the train in that part of the city at night. And the walk, or climb, was special, in its way. A descent, in a sense, but a descent into something familiar. He would reach his destination, and the train would stop. He would rest, stop, for awhile, and then walk, or climb, to the bottom of the hill. He would stand in the backyard. The light was on, or there was a yellow light bulb in the backyard. The yellow light attracted bugs, or insects, many, many bugs, or insects.

The funeral had required a great deal of planning, in fact, arrangements had to be made in advance.

There was a bug, or insect, in the room. For once, or on this occasion, a bug, or insect, had followed him inside. A bug, or insect, had made its way into the room where he stood. However, the room was never silent. There was often noise, one form of noise or another, that would, inevitably, bother him. Yet, it was usually quiet in the neighborhood, in that neighborhood, in that part of the city, at night. And he had, in fact, walked, or climbed, a long ways down.

———

Arrangements for the funeral were made by _____ _____.

———

The café was crowded. His friends, associates, sat at a table and talked. The cemetery was in the middle of the city, not far from the café.

———

And the funeral had, in fact, been a success, well planned, well attended. A success, in a sense, as far as funerals go.

———

It had been long, a long time, since he'd visited that neighborhood, that part of the city, the backyard, at night. Still, the neighborhood, that neighborhood, that part of the city, the backyard, was much the same. He exited the train station and walked, or climbed, down a steep hill. The train station sat on a hill, high on a hill, and he would get off the train and walk, or climb, each night in his dream, walk, or climb, through that part of the city. That part of the city was lush, wild, unkempt, a jungle, in its way.

———

He sat at a table at the café, or restaurant. The café was crowded that afternoon. Still, the weather was fine. The weather was good, and many people sat in cafés and restaurants.

———

He saw his friends, associates, approach the café door. He waved, gestured, with his hands, somewhat wildly, did a kind of dance, almost a dance, trying to get their attention. However, he was not certain that they had seen him. He was running a bit late that day. He'd been running late more and more frequently, then, at that point. And he was usually on time when he had a plan, an arrangement, to meet with someone.

Indeed, very little of what he did actually say during their conversation could be heard across the table. It was crowded and, more or less, noisy in the restaurant that evening. And the waiter took their orders.

And his walk, or climb, downhill would often begin late at night. He was, however, not afraid to walk alone at night. It was a descent, yes, in a sense, but a descent into something familiar. And walking, or climbing, in general, was good, was, generally, believed to be good exercise, at that point.

It was still light out, at that point, still daytime, as he stood on the street, not far from the café, and waited.

Even though it was dark, he was immediately able to recognize where he was. He was in the neighborhood, in that neighborhood, in that part of the city, in the backyard at night. And the neighborhood, that neighborhood, the backyard, that part of the city, was lush. In fact it was a jungle compared to where he lived now. In the city.

And, from time to time, he could hear the sound of the train, the sound of trains, or the train station, all through the neighborhood, that neighborhood, that part of the city, the backyard at night.

The city itself was built on a series of hills. Yet, the hills the city was built on are, for the most part, small and insignificant. It is easy to forget that the city is set on a series of hills, except on certain streets, and in certain neighborhoods, where the hills are, more or less, noticeable.

The cemetery is set on a hill, high on a hill. And the hill is, for the most part, fairly large, or high. The cemetery itself is pleasant, in a way, a pleasant place, for the most part. There is, indeed, a somewhat pleasant aspect to the cemetery, and this pleasant aspect is a credit, a lasting monument, if you will, to those who participated in the cemetery's original construction and design.

14

There was light, and there was air, for the most part, from what he could see through the windows, through the trees.

———

The arrangements had been made ahead of time. Indeed, the funeral had been planned, planned well in advance.

———

There is something about the summer air, the spring air, the winter air, the autumn air, he feels. He is riding the train to the station. When he reaches the station, he will exit the train and walk, climb, down a steep hill and through the neighborhood, that neighborhood, that part of the city, where it is lush, and where there are many trees.

———

His friends, associates, sit at a table in the café and talk. It has been a long day: the funeral and the walk to the café and the sitting at the table and the toasts and the drinking of a variety of beverages and everything else.

———

It is too early to tell, still too early to tell, how it will all play out. He is not sure, but he is hopeful, sometimes, and, at other times, less hopeful. Still, the trees are most splendid at night, he feels.

It is nighttime and beautiful and he is crossing the street. He is in a different part of the city. The train station is, at that point, quite a distance away. The train station sits at the top of a hill, or, rather, he has walked, or climbed, down a steep hill. He is crossing the street and he notices the trees and plants and flowers, all the life of the city, that part of the city. And the life of the city, that part of the city, is rich, lush, compared to where he lives now. In the city. And the world is, more or less, different there, he feels. And this thought gives him a chill, sends a, rather, unique sensation, or charge, throughout his body. And, thus, he is confused. He can't, in fact, be certain anymore. Suddenly, it seems that it is hard for him to concentrate. And then there is a memory, a memory of a particular time and place. An engine. There is an engine, or the sound of an engine of some sort, working.

———

He is standing in the middle of the street, on the concrete pedestrian island in the middle of the street. It is daytime, and he has a meeting scheduled, or he is supposed to be meeting his friends, associates, at a café.

———

She has not arrived for their meeting. He is not quite certain what time it is. He is not sure if she is late, or if he is early, or if he is late. There is a name on the green, or red, door, or not a name exactly, but a mark, a specific mark, or some kind of sign, or symbol. He pushes the door, though he knows the door is, in fact, locked. The door is locked, again and again, but he must get inside. He is curious, certain, about what might be in the room. The door is locked, kept shut, with a chain and padlock. It is a green, or red, door. The door to a storage cellar that is used by the café next door. And perhaps he should call her on the telephone.

———

He is walking. It is a cold day, or it is a very warm day, or it is in the cool of the evening after an uncharacteristically warm day that he takes his walk, usually takes his walks.

———

There is not a cloud in the sky. It is a beautiful day, and there is not any reason to rush, not specifically, although his friends, associates, are, at that point, more or less, relieved to be exiting the cemetery.

———

His friends, associates, sit at a table in the café and eat and talk and drink a variety of beverages. And there are tentative plans, or arrangements, made for them to meet again, to meet at another time, though, perhaps, in a different location.

———

The day has been long. The trees and plants and flowers are beautiful, and he feels that there is much to be grateful for, much to be thankful for. And then he stands in the backyard. There are bugs, or insects, many, many bugs, or insects, in the backyard. On this night, the bugs, or insects, are especially noisy, especially active. The weather has changed, and then changed again. At this time the weather is warmer, much warmer, than it has been for some time. And it is almost like a dream. The time has passed by very quickly. What began as a spur of the moment decision to ride the train to the station has become something of a routine. And he is, typically, the only one left on the train when it reaches that particular station.

———

151

And it is strange, after all, in a way, very strange, that the funeral has been so well planned. There are many guests, friends, associates, and relatives, and others, other people who attend the funeral. Friends, associates, and relatives, and others, unknown others, strangers, in a sense, who attend the funeral. There are flowers and there is a casket. There is an open grave, a gravesite. And planning the funeral has been a hard and difficult process. No one can deny that planning the funeral has been a hard and difficult process. Even then, there might have been a place for the mourners to go, to meet, after the funeral, that is, the friends, associates, and relatives, and others, the others who have attended the funeral. Still, it is after the funeral and everyone leaves the cemetery, walks across the long expanse of grass in an orderly, dignified, and respectful manner.

It is a beautiful evening. He is standing in the backyard and he hears something, some unknown sound. And there are affirmations, he feels, in every sound he hears, especially in the sounds the walls make, in the sounds of the wood, and also in the sounds of the ceiling. And it is strange to be sitting there, after all, very strange, and, somewhat, unexpected.

It is night, or it is morning, or it is afternoon.

And the time, or time, in general, then, at that point, made very little difference. He is walking on the streets of the city alone.

He was late. Or she was early. And he saw them. At that point, he was certain that he saw his friends, associates, approach the café from the sidewalk.

———

And the café is crowded that day.

———

His friends, associates, many of them, have come from a long ways away. They have sat together at the table and have talked and have consumed a variety of beverages.

———

He is standing on the street. He is standing in the middle of the street. Still, there is no reason to panic, even if he is a little late. He checks his watch, tries to check his watch, but it is not there, at that point, not on his wrist, and not in his pockets. He has forgotten that it has been some time since he has paid attention to his watch, some time since he has stopped wearing a watch. And it would be a painful reminder, his watch would be, anyway, if it were there, on his wrist, he feels.

———

There are many trees in the cemetery, standing, here and there, on the long expanse of grass. And the cemetery itself exists as a sort of reminder, a reminder of, in a sense, a bygone era. The city once was lush and green and there were trees and plants and flowers everywhere. The cemetery is surrounded by a wrought iron gate, by a red brick wall. And everyone thinks of a bygone era, in one way or another, as they walk or drive by the cemetery. The cemetery is old and has high walls. There are trees and plants and flowers that grow, in places, lushly, all over the red brick wall, and all over the wrought iron gate. And the cemetery is, in fact, more or less, picturesque, unique, pleasant, in its way.

Postscript - Night

The scene is set in the city. The scene is set in an apartment, or in a caféteria, or in a bar, warehouse, restaurant, or on the street. There are no snakes or deer or bears on the fence. There is nothing particularly funny or clever to relate to his friends, not then, definitely not at that point, he feels. But within the room it is easy to find a desk. It is easy to find chairs. It is easy to find the things that almost anyone in any circumstance might need to feel comfortable. There is even a bed. It is the middle of the night and the man rises, puts his shoes on, or, rather, he gets out of bed.

The scene with the doctor takes place in a room in the city. And, at that point, he is almost in tears. The man is in a room in the city and he has to have himself checked. He is at the doctor's office and he is almost in tears.

The scene takes place in a doctor's office. The doctor is an old man. The doctor asks him specific questions, the typical questions a doctor might ask.

It is the middle of the night, and the man wakes up and coughs, or clears his throat. The cough, or, rather, the excessive amount of phlegm in his throat, is part of his condition, his serious condition, he feels. He has just had a nightmare, or, rather, he has just woken up in the middle of the night from a persistent and irritating cough.

The condition is not contagious, and it is not progressive, but the condition will not improve in any meaningful way for the rest of his life. Or so the doctor tells him.

The doctor tells the man he is ill.

There was a building near the apartment house that had blown up. A commercial building. The building was old, but was very much still in use, and it had blown up in the middle of the night.

A large explosion rocked the city. But the explosion, the one that had destroyed the commercial building, had sounded more like air being sucked in, a sharp intake of air, like someone dying.

He was asleep and the sound of an explosion woke him,

waking up to the horrible sound of something exploding, the sound, or non-sound, of air being sucked in, like a machine, perhaps, running in reverse, or someone dying.

And very soon after, there were sirens. And then the scene changed, or, rather, moved. At first an explosion, or the sound, or non-sound, of air being sucked in, like something, a mechanism, perhaps, running in reverse, and then several minutes of silence, and then sirens, or, rather, the arrival of the proper authorities. The explosion occurred in the middle of the night and robbed him of his sleep. But beyond that, beyond that particular incident, there were other forces to contend with, other manifestations of authority that required his attention.

The commercial building had been one of the older ones in the neighborhood. It had been large and had occupied an entire corner: small storefronts at street level, a warehouse space in back, off the alley, and offices, mostly medical offices, on the upper floors.

The explosion, at least preliminarily, of course, could have happened anywhere. It could have occurred in a similar way in a department store or in a prison or in a laboratory, he feels.

A figure stood on the street and waited. There was a figure, a man, on the street, close to the corner, that stood and waited for him to approach.

It was the middle of the night and there was a song playing on the radio, a popular song. There were plates and containers of half-eaten food on the table and there were men talking and playing cards in the backroom of the warehouse. And one wanted a song in those days, especially under those circumstances. Still, it might have been better if someone had been there to wait with him. The pressure might have eased considerably. And, in the end, if only the radio in the warehouse had been tuned to a news station instead, an all-news station, the waiting might have been much less harmful and confusing.

The man he was expected to meet carried a small transistor radio.

The radio was to be set to a station that played popular music, an all popular music station, but he hadn't paid attention to music in years, and he would be required to listen for specific music, recognize specific popular songs on the radio.

He stood on the corner in his overcoat and waited in the rain. The fear, the level of fear, was incredible, and intoxicating, too, in its way.

It was silver, thin, and very small. The radio was carefully tucked beneath the man's left arm.

The city was cold and damp. The city was wet in the rain. The light was bad. The light was dark and almost non-existent.

And how would the radio play in the rain?

And if he couldn't recognize the popular songs that played on the radio, what would happen next?

Talking to the man in the car. He was talking to the driver, and he was very afraid that he would say something inadvertently. He was very afraid that he would stand in the rain and, perhaps, say something out of turn.

In the building there was a man.

The man who owned the building was very old by then, and he didn't much care about the building, except, of course, on the days he would come to collect the rent.

The owner of the building was dead. He was dead and gone, and then, one night, the building disappeared. A large explosion rocked the city.

The noise from the radio continued to bother the neighbors. He'd sat in his room and waited. He'd waited and waited, trying to identify as many popular songs that played on the radio as he could, until it was time to go.

The apartment building was at the end of the street. He lived in a small apartment in the city.

157

He was, at that point, supposed to meet a man on the corner. He stood on the corner and waited, but it was raining and the man he was expected to meet was supposed to be holding a radio. A small transistor radio was supposed to be playing one of three specific popular songs. When one of the three specific songs began playing, he was supposed to approach the man. There was supposed to be an exchange made.

The apartment house is very large and old and has been there for as long as anyone can remember. It sits at the end of a cul-de-sac and looks rather ominous, and very desolate, especially at night.

One night, the man comes home and walks up the hall that leads to his apartment door.

He knows then, at that point, that that he has, indeed, been very successful, and, thus, there will be a change.

A change is coming very soon, immediately, in fact. He is sure.

And once inside of his apartment, the man will sit in a comfortable chair and light a cigarette. He will read a newspaper. Later, he will make something to eat. And once, when the man was young, he would listen to the radio at night. He would hide under the blankets and listen to popular songs on the radio.

As expected, the hall is dark. He has finally reached his apartment door, and the hall is dark. However, the key to his apartment door is in his hand.

And, yet, there is still much to consider, he feels. There are various wires and switches and other materials currently housed in a warehouse somewhere in the city, and there are the plans and the various other documents, and there are other important successes to be achieved as well.

There was a great tree that stood in front of the apartment building when he'd first moved in. The tree was very tall and old and the upper branches covered his apartment window. The tree provided comfort and beauty and privacy. And then the tree was gone. One day when he returned home from work, the tree was gone.

An empty vase stood by a door in the hall, and a pair of muddy shoes stood in front of another door, and an unread newspaper was in front of yet another door.

He was holding a key in his hand, the key to his apartment door, when the lights in the hall went out.

The man covers his ears with his hands, closes his eyes, briefly, and then, in a flash, the world changes, or, rather, moves, becomes something else entirely.

A wrong look, or maybe someone staring at him while he ate dinner at the caféteria, or, perhaps, while he ate lunch in a café, or restaurant.

The air was thin and foggy.

The air was damp and foggy.

He'd stood on the corner and waited. He'd waited and waited.

He remembered standing on the corner and waiting. Why, it had been just yesterday when he'd stood on the corner and waited in the rain. And it hadn't been at all long ago when he'd stood on a corner and waited in the rain.

It did, however, occur to him, at one point, to ask for help. It should have been easy to find a telephone. It should have been easy to pick up the telephone and call for help. There were people, associates, contacts, who were supposed to help you when things went wrong. One did not have to do everything alone. Indeed, it was something he'd have to remember in the future.

He stood in line with his tray at the caféteria and waited to pay for his food. The man in front of him in line purchased a small carton of milk and rubbed his eye with a handkerchief. Apparently there was something in the man's eye that bothered him.

He sat in the caféteria and ate.

He would often eat his lunch in a café, or restaurant.

He is eating dinner in the caféteria, and there is a cup of soup and a tray on the table in front of him.

The caféteria is on a street in the city. He is eating soup and there is no one to talk to and nothing to read.

The telephone rings.

He is in his apartment when the telephone rings.

It is the middle of the night and he has just fallen asleep when the telephone begins to ring.

One night he leaves his apartment and walks on the streets of the city. There is a great deal of pressure in the air, and the pressure seems to have directed itself exclusively to his solar plexus by the time he reaches the warehouse.

There is a game going on in the backroom, and there is great deal of laughter among the men. The men are taking inventory that night. He must step carefully, noiselessly around the boxes and pallets. He must be especially careful not to trip or make a sound as he passes near the backroom.

There is a game going on in the backroom and the warehouse is filled with boxes that must be counted, or, rather, accounted for that night.

The neighborhood is quiet, as it always is at that time of night. The neighborhood is quiet and he is climbing the stairs. He is thinking first, briefly, of his teeth and how he must go to the dentist as soon as he has time. Then he is thinking about what he'd overheard during the game in the backroom of the warehouse. He climbs the stairs and reaches his floor. He enters the hall that leads to the door of his apartment. Halfway across the hall, he takes his keys out of his pocket, and then the lights go out.

He is walking home to his apartment. Earlier that night, he'd waited in the rain for hours. He'd been standing on the corner when it started to rain. There was supposed to have been a man waiting for him. The man was supposed to have been holding a small transistor radio.

He looked at himself in the window of a car parked on the

street. He stood in front of his apartment building and saw himself reflected in the glass front doors. The building stood at the end of a cul-de-sac and looked large, and desolate, and somewhat ominous, as it always did at night.

As he approached his apartment door, he wondered if it was still raining outside.

He'd been feeling well that day. He'd seen a doctor. It was windy on the street that night. He hummed a popular tune. He was walking on the streets of the city, not far from his apartment. The building was large and old and sat at the end of a cul-de-sac. However, the windows were not lit in his apartment. Perhaps, he'd forgotten to turn on the lights before he'd left earlier that evening.

The man who had been standing in front of him in line at the cafeteria approached him. The man asked if the empty seat at his table was taken.

The cafeteria often played popular music through loudspeakers that were mounted on the walls.

The café played music on a radio that was kept behind the bar.

He hummed a popular tune as he stood in the hall.

A man had confronted him in the cafeteria. The man had said something to him. He had asked if the empty seat at his table was taken. And there had been any number of people in the cafeteria at the time. It was lunchtime in the cafeteria.

He climbed the staircase and looked at the cracks in the paint on the wall. He walked down the hall that lead to his apartment door and thought about the cracks in the paint on the stairway wall. How run-down the apartment building was becoming. The elevator had been broken for months. He took out his keys.

A man stood in front of him in the cafeteria. The man in the cafeteria moved, more or less, quickly. He'd woken up in the middle of the night. He'd had a bad dream, or, rather, a nightmare. The man in the cafeteria had asked him if the empty seat at his table was taken. As he approached his apartment door, the light in the hall went off.

The man at the caféteria seemed to move, more or less, quickly.

He held the key to his apartment in his hand.

He often carried his key in his hand, or, rather, in his fist with the sharp point sticking out, in the manner of a weapon. In fact, he often carried his key with the sharp point jutting from his fist, in the manner of a weapon, when he walked home to his apartment building at night.

Acknowledgements

Excerpts from *Blind Spot* have appeared in *Anomalous Press* and *Sidebrow*. Thank you to the generous editors of these publications.

Thank you Amanda Ackerman, Allison Carter, Dan Richert, Janet Sarbanes, Veronica Gonzalez, Danielle Dutton, and TC Tolbert.

Thank you Andrea Quaid.

Thank you Sean Pessin, Teresa Carmody, Nadu Barbashova, and Andrew Wessels.

Thank you Harriet, Theodore, Sharone Abramowitz, and Nathan Abramowitz.

Thank you Michael Seidlinger.

And super special thanks to Janice Lee for all her loving support of this work, and everything else, too.

———

The Editor would like to thank Kirk Myers at the Pasadena Musem of History and John Venegas.

OFFICIAL

CCM ◐

GET OUT OF JAIL
* VOUCHER *

- -

Tear this out.
Skip that social event.
It's okay.
You don't have to go if you don't want to. Pick up
the book you just bought. Open to the first page.
You'll thank us by the third paragraph.

If friends ask why you were a no-show, show them
this voucher.
You'll be fine.

- - - - - - - - - - - - - - - - - - - -

We're coping.

◐

CPSIA information can be obtained
at www.ICGtesting.com
Printed in the USA
FSOW02n0900170816
23880FS